CCS Investigations

Book Two : The Chosen

By

Susan Elle

For

Ursula Publishing UK

CCS Investigations

Book Two : The Chosen

Text Copyright © 2013

By Susan Elle

Ursula Publishing UK

All Rights Reserved.

Cover Photograph

© Rido/Dreamstime.com

ISBN 978-1-910753-12-5

Other Books by Susan Elle

The Sara Colson Trilogy includes
Sara's Child
Sara's Loss
Sara's Shame
All the above also available as audio books.

Catherine Colson-Sayers Investigations
CCS Investigations : Bk 1 : Missing
CCS Investigations : Bk 2 : The Chosen
CCS Investigations : Bk 3 : Travis
CCS Investigations : Bk 4 : Deleted
CCS Investigations : Bk 5 : Mind Games, due out end
Aug 2015, twice the length of previous books.

Tempest
Broken

Love, Lies & Consequences Trilogy
Book One : Love
Book Two : Lies
Book Three : Consequences

http://www.susan-elle.com/

Table of Contents

PROLOGUE

In a large forbidding house, that seems bereft of soul, lays a young woman with the weight of the world pressing heavily in on her chest.

Rain is pounding at the windows and she can hear the wind tossed trees thrashing their branches against the house.

If that were all she could hear, Jessie would thank her lucky stars, but it isn't.

Above the storm she can hear the sounds of terrible suffering.

"Please, Jessie...please help me. Don't leave me like this, I can't bear it anymore. Aaahh, God take me, please take me..."

Her mother has been in pain for what seems like forever. The diagnosis of her cancer had been hampered by the fact that their doctor hadn't bothered to send her mother to the hospital. He'd insisted that a course of anti-inflammatory medication would ease the pain.

In the end it had been a locum who had been called out twice, when the pain had become unbearable, who had called an ambulance to get her mother into the hospital.

It hadn't taken long for the cancer to be diagnosed and pronounced inoperable.

And Jessie had seen for herself the suffering of the people there, the way the doctors and nurses just allowed it to continue.

That's why I brought you home, mother. But even the Oramorph isn't keeping the pain away for long now. I can't do what you want, mother, I don't want to lose you.

But then...I'm being just like those doctors and those nurses, swanning around making decisions about people's lives – 'No, I'm afraid you can't have any more pain medication just now, it isn't time for the drug round yet'; and just like that another person is left to suffer like a dog.

Yes, just like a dog...they put dogs down, don't they? If a dog is in pain and suffering, they put the dog down.

"Jessie please, I can't take this anymore. Let me go, baby. Please...help me to go."

"I'm right here, mother. I'm right here," and she walks into her mother's bedroom.

Taking a seat on the bed, Jessie leans forward to stroke her mother's brow. "It's alright, mother, I'm right here."

"Please, Jessie, I know you're frightened of being left on your own..." her mother gasps as the pain rips through her again, "...please...I need your help. I need you...to let me go."

"I love you, mother," Jessie tells her, continuing to stroke her mother's hair from her face. "You know I'd do anything to take away your pain, but what you're asking..."

Taking her daughter's hand with her frail, trembling one, Mavis Pearson looks deep into her daughter's troubled eyes.

"Is it wrong to end this terrible suffering?" she asks, gasping and gripping Jessie's hand as her pain mounts. "You...you need to...to be strong for me...my angel."

Bringing her mother's hand to her lips, Jessie looks back at her with tears flowing freely down her cheeks and nods.

Taking the pillow lying next to her mother she asks, "Are you sure?"

Nodding, Mavis closes her eyes and lays as still and as quiet as the pain allows knowing that, at last, the pain will end. *Please, my brave angel, set me free.*

Moving the pillow to cover her mother's pain ravaged face, Jessie holds it in place then presses gently but firmly.

She doesn't struggle or cry out, and doesn't take long to die.

Outside the storm continues to rage...but in the large dark house, death is silent...final...and an 'angel of death' is born!

Removing the pillow, Jessie looks down at her mother's peaceful face and sobs.

"Why...why did you make me do this?" Stroking her mother's hair, she can already feel the warmth leaving her lifeless body. "They should have helped you; they should have given you better medicine to take the pain away. I hate them for what they did to you. I hate them all!"

Drawing up the duvet, Jessie covers her mother as if she is only sleeping.

"Goodnight, mother. Sleep well...I'll see you in the morning."

CHAPTER ONE

"No, no, yes, that's it," Catherine tells the man who is trying to position her desk in the new home office that she and Emma will share. "Now just take it back about a foot and it will be perfect," she smiles, happy to see her plans coming together.

"I could have done this all for you," Logan offers, watching his wife try not to become frazzled by the task in hand.

"And what would be the point in that...," she asks him, "...I'd only have to move it all around again to get things how I want them."

Conceding the point, Logan decides to stand back and let Catherine continue to direct operations as long as she doesn't try moving or lifting anything herself.

Even at 33 weeks pregnant, he wouldn't put it past

her to do more than she should.

I think I'll go grey before our boys arrive, she just can't not try to do things by herself. Miss Independent! But then, Catherine was fiercely independent when we met, I can't expect her to change overnight.

Smiling, he watches her nod and smile then shake her head and redirect someone in placing a printer where she wants it.

"Ok, time for a break," Logan taps Catherine on the shoulder and gets a frown of dissent for his trouble. "No good looking like that. Everything that needs to be placed has been, the rest is just fiddling," he tells her, and guides Catherine out of the room, much to the workmen's relief.

"Got your bossy head on today," Catherine grumbles as they walk into the conservatory. "You can always go into work if you feel like throwing your weight around."

"I was not throwing my weight around," he protests with a raised brow. "And I'm staying right here to keep an eye on you."

"I knew that's what you were doing," Catherine frowns up at him grumpily. "I'm not a child, Logan. I can look after myself!"

"That's debateable," he laughs, tipping her chin up to place a kiss on her lips.

"I've brought a nice cup of tea for you both," and Mrs

Baines sets a tray down in front of them.

"Thanks," Catherine says, a little ungraciously, then smiles in spite of herself when she spots her favourite choc-chip biscuits. "You're a gem, Mrs B!"

"You spoil her," Logan frowns playfully. "But I suppose there's no harm in it."

However, when he makes to take one of the biscuits for himself, Catherine swiftly bats his hand away.

"Mine!" she yelps, and snatches the little plate away. "Go get your own!"

Chuckling deeply, Logan watches Catherine chomp happily on the biscuits, relishing every bite.

"I swear you've got even more of a sweet tooth since you've been pregnant. I'm not sure that's a good thing, but it is good to see you eating again," he tells her with a contented nod.

"I don't know why I've been off my food again," Catherine muses as she finishes the last biscuit. "I think the boys are taking up so much room, I just don't really get hungry."

"Hmm, well, you're going to have to force something down," Logan warns her. "Apart from the pregnancy there's not a lot of weight on you."

"Well that's good, isn't it?" she asks with a lift of her chin. "At least you won't be stuck with a fat wife after I've given birth!"

"That is hardly a concern…," Logan tells her reproachfully, "…but your health is. And I see nothing wrong with my woman having a few more curves – I can never get enough of you as it is."

And truth be told, neither of them has found their sex drive hampered by her pregnancy. If anything, Catherine sometimes feels she wants Logan even more. Her body seems so alive, so sensitive to his touch. He can make her shudder with just a look and frazzle her brain with a simple touch.

Watching her, it's as if Logan can read her mind. His breath quickens as he watches Catherine's thoughts play across her face.

"Let's go for a walk," and he grabs her hand while opening the patio doors.

When they reach the fishpond, Logan steers her to the bench and takes a seat beside her.

"What was that all about?" Catherine asks.

"Just needed a breath of fresh air," Logan tells her, filling his lungs with the stuff.

"You were getting horny," Catherine chuckles knowingly.

"Well if I was it was your fault," Logan frowns down at her. "You should have seen your face – the way you were looking at me I knew exactly what you were thinking. So don't play the innocent," he tells her.

"Actually, I was just thinking about what I want to do to you when those pesky workmen of yours finally disappear." Putting a hand to his chest, she pops a shirt button and slips it inside.

Feeling his heart beat jump wildly, Catherine lets out a sexy chuckle.

"See, you want me just as much," she smiles wickedly.

"Which is why we're out here!" Logan claps a hand over Catherine's, trying to stem the lust she is stirring in him.

"As I recall, we had wonderful sex in the garden not so long ago," Catherine teases.

"But the house wasn't full of people," Logan states, then takes a long slow breath. "Now behave yourself or I'll make love to you right here, audience be damned!"

Catherine sits up, wide eyed and unsure if he's teasing. "You wouldn't!"

But the look he gives her causes Catherine to swallow hard.

"That's better...," Logan chides her, "...now be a good girl and feed the fish."

He watches as Catherine gets up and pushes the plunger in to get a palm full of pellets from the dispenser nearby.

"You and Charlie are becoming good friends," Logan observes with a grin, remembering when the Koi Carp's habit of jumping almost clear of the water had frightened Catherine and her sister, Caroline.

"I know when you're laughing at me," Catherine tells him with only a mild rebuke in her voice. "But I don't care, anyone would have screamed when a fish the size of Charlie almost takes their hand off!"

Laughing now, Logan moves to stand beside his wife and put an arm across her shoulders. "I came running to your rescue, as I remember."

Looking sidelong up at him, Catherine recalls the moment clearly. "As I remember you also split your sides laughing," Catherine recalls, and can't stem the smile that tugs at her lips.

"You have to admit, it was pretty funny," Logan hugs her shoulders and places a kiss on the top of her head.

"I suppose," she admits. "But, Jesus, I've never seen a fish the size of Charlie. Are you sure he isn't eating his companions? I swear there are less of them now than when I moved in here!"

Chuckling, Logan shakes his head, "There are more, actually." Guiding her round the pond he points to a jet black shadow and further out to a pure gold monster gliding through the water.

"Jesus, Logan! Are you sure that one isn't a shark!?" she asks, pointing to the black shape swimming away from them.

"No...," he smiles happily, "...he's definitely a very large Koi Carp, and he cost me a pretty penny I can tell you."

Catherine frowns, watching the shadow swim away. "What will you do when we move to Lakelands?"

"I've already got that in hand," he tells her. "At the same time as digging out the swimming pool, I've asked the builders to dig out a large enough pond for the fish to move into."

"You've really thought about all this," Catherine smiles up at her husband, glad that he is easy with the move back home to Lakelands and his father, Henry.

Giving her shoulders another hug, Logan smiles down at her and loves what he sees in her eyes. *You have so much love in that huge heart of yours, if only you wouldn't hide it from the rest of the world!*

"You haven't talked me into anything that I'm not happy to do. So stop worrying," he tells her kindly. "I think raising our boys at Lakelands will be precious, and my father will love the chance to be a hands-on grandad."

"Well, look at you...," an accusatory voice breaks into their conversation, "...and here I thought I'd find you orchestrating the set-up like a sergeant major!"

Logan smiles a welcome and tells Emma that she isn't far off the mark. "That's exactly what she was doing until I lead her away for a break."

"Well it looks great," Emma smiles and nods her approval. "Looks like we've got plenty of room to move, and I saw the white-boards you've had put up on a couple of the walls – a great way to brainstorm."

"Yes, and I've got boxes of small magnets that we can use to pin information to them, which will allow us to move it around as and when we need to," Catherine enthuses, her brain kicking into work mode.

Logan knows when he's fighting a losing battle, and decides that their restful walk in the garden is over for now.

"If you girls want to discuss work, I'm going to get some of my own done," he smiles, dipping his head to give Catherine a kiss before he moves back indoors.

"He is such a great catch," Emma observes while watching Logan's retreat. "He not only 'get's you', that man is an orgasm on legs - or stilts in Logan's case," she chuckles, then turns to see Catherine regarding her darkly.

"Joking!" Emma states, holding her hands up in surrender. "Well, mostly. But you have to admit, he is hot!

And the way his tight arse moves in those fitted trousers-"

"Stop, now!" Catherine warns. "Drooling over my husband is not in your contract, so get over it!"

"Can't I just have a little drool as long as I keep my lusty thoughts to myself?" Emma begs, watching as Logan steps inside the conservatory and out of view.

Frowning deeply, Catherine knows her new colleague is joking, but only just. "I thought you were seeing that detective with the weird name? What's up isn't he doing it for you?"

"Sloane is a stickler for the rules," she tells Catherine. "We had an argument about the agency we're starting up and the tactics we're likely to employ."

Catherine actually laughs and shakes her head. "So he doesn't like the idea of you using your mad computer skills to hack into places," she guesses correctly, and watches Emma's frown deepen.

"He can be so damned self-righteous!" she huffs as they follow Logan back into the house. "I told him to climb down off his high horse and get real. We helped put a stop to the torture and slaughter of innocent couples. Something that may not have happened if we hadn't intervened!"

"Oh boy, I bet he loved hearing that," Catherine chuckles as they make their way up to their new office.

"As a matter of fact, he didn't," and Emma takes a seat behind the desk that already has her laptop stationed on it. "He said we were irresponsible meddlers, though he did concede that we were doing it with the best of intentions!"

"Looking at your face, and the fact that you sound like you're ready to punch his lights out, I'd say that conversation didn't end well," Catherine observes, concerned for her new friend.

"Let's just say, he's no big loss," Emma continues to frown as she opens her laptop and fires it up. "Damned copper! Who needs a man anyway – they just screw with your head!"

Catherine is wise enough to know when to stay silent, and moves to fire up her laptop.

"I mean, who set him up as moral judge and jury – just because he's got a damn badge," Emma continues to rant, not really speaking to Catherine now. "What we did was awesome and that's what sticks in his craw! We did what they couldn't – and we'll do it again!"

Now Catherine can hear the feverish dance of Emma's fingers on her keyboard and knows that her mad hasn't passed yet.

"What gives Sloane Shivers the right to put us down?" she asks no one in particular. "I mean, you don't see

Logan having a hissy fit every time you open your laptop –
so why can't Sloane just back off and leave us to do what
we do?"

Remembering some of Logan's reactions to what she
had done in the past, Catherine feels it's time to come
clean.

"Actually-"

But Emma hasn't finished, and gets up to pace off
some of her pent up frustrations. "Logan is so cool – you
need to count yourself lucky to have found such a gem.
Some men are just so far up their own backsides they
can't see past the shit to their brains!"

Catherine quickly moves to shield her boys ears by
placing firm hands at either side of her stomach but
decides not to interrupt Emma's flow, figuring that her
mad will burn out quicker if she just let's her vent.

"Even Frank tried to reason with him," Emma
declares, as if that was vindication in itself. "I mean, he's
probably twice Sloane's age yet he's open minded enough
to realise that we can do a lot of good with our unique
skills."

"He actually said that?" Catherine asks, somewhat
surprised.

Emma comes to a stop in front of Catherine's desk
and nods enthusiastically. "He did! Maybe I should be

dating Frank instead of that dick-head partner of his!"

"So, you are still dating Sloane?" Catherine asks tentatively.

"I suppose so. I don't know," Emma frowns, retaking her seat and boring holes into her screen with a++ fierce glare.

"Is that all that's bothering you?" Catherine asks, concerned at the level of Emma's anger.

Putting her elbows on her desk, Emma drops her face into her hands and takes a deep, steadying breath.

"My favourite aunt died a few days ago," she sighs and lifts her head to look over at Catherine. "She was so vital, so full of energy and had a real love of life. It doesn't seem possible that she's gone – just like that, she isn't there anymore..."

Not used to dealing with people or their emotions, Catherine hesitates to respond, not wanting to say the wrong thing and make Emma feel even worse.

"So...you were close?"

"Very. When I left home to go to uni' she became my surrogate mother as she lived nearby." Then Emma's face lights up with a memory. "I could tell her anything, aunt Izzy never sat in judgement – not like some people," Emma adds, though her smile doesn't fade.

"Izzy...?" Catherine frowns.

"Isabelle, but she hated the formality of her name so she never used it," Emma explains. "Aunt Izzy was the very opposite of formal. Whenever I needed a friend's ear, she was always there. I could just drop in at a moment's notice and bend her ear about anything; boys, sex...she even knew about my hacking days," Emma grins wickedly.

"And she was ok with it?" Catherine asks with a raised brow.

"More than," Emma giggles girlishly. "Aunt Izzy was so cool; she just warned me to be careful then asked for all the details."

"Wow, she really was cool," Catherine smiles in amazement.

"Yeah, she really was," Emma agrees, her voice low and thoughtful.

For a moment Catherine hesitates, then asks, "So what did the doctors say about your aunt?"

Frowning, Emma remembers the conversation she'd had with her aunt's consultant.

"They admitted it wasn't an outcome they had foreseen," she tells Catherine. "It was just a broken hip. Izzy took a spill in the garden and ended up in the hospital. But no one ever said her condition was life threatening," Emma explains, having to wipe away an errant tear.

"So, the surgery went well?" Catherine asks.

Nodding vigorously, Emma looks across at Catherine with a sudden smile. "You would never have guessed she'd had major surgery – aunt Izzy was sitting up, bright as a button when I last saw her. That's what's so devastating – I didn't see it coming, and neither did the doctors from what they told me."

"Hmm..." Catherine muses, not saying anything more.

"I was probably more angry with Sloane than he deserved," Emma says, reflecting on their last meeting. "It was the day after Izzy passed; I wasn't feeling at my best."

"And that idiot, Shivers, was dumb enough to get on your case!" Catherine states angrily. "He deserved what he got!"

Smiling at her friend's umbrage on her behalf, Emma shakes her head. "No, he really didn't. He doesn't know about Izzy, I was still too raw to talk about it."

"Oh. Well, he still shouldn't have been so off with you," Catherine tells her, loyalty colouring her opinion.

"Thanks. I don't know if I'll get the chance to explain now. I pretty much told him to sod off," she admits with a grimace.

Not sure how to comfort her friend, Catherine decides to distract her with work.

"You know you're the one who's going on the PI

course," she states suddenly, totally throwing Emma off her thoughts.

"What? What PI course?" Emma asks nonplussed.

"Oh, I thought I'd mentioned it," Catherine frowns, looking through a box of papers. "Here," she offers, thrusting a hand holding an A4 envelope out in Emma's general direction.

Getting up, Emma takes the envelope and studies its contents. "This looks really interesting..." she states, looking over at Catherine, "...are you sure you don't want to do this? We could do it together."

Catherine's grimace speaks volumes. "That would mean being polite to a whole bunch of people that I don't know from Adam! And then there's the tea-breaks and lunch times – having to sit with people and make civil conversation."

Shaking her head Catherine's grimace deepens. "Nope, you go for it. You can fill me in on anything you think I need to know."

Chuckling softly, Emma shakes her head. "You can pretend to be a Grinch if you want, but I know there's a nice side to you."

"Then you're delusional," Catherine states without a hint of a smile. "Now get on with some work or I'll fire you on your first day!"

Not the least bit intimidated, Emma crosses back to her desk and continues reading about the PI course.

However, Catherine isn't taking any notice. She's just hacked into the medical records of Emma's aunt Izzy.

CHAPTER TWO

"Logan, I'm telling you, there was nothing in her notes to indicate that Isabelle was anything but on the road to being discharged," Catherine insists over breakfast in the conservatory next morning.

"So, what are you saying, that someone made a mistake and Isabelle died? That sounds a bit far-fetched," Logan frowns into his bacon and eggs doubtfully.

"I'm not sure what I'm saying at this point," Catherine admits. "But even the doctors were perplexed by her death. It said as much in the last entry in her medical notes."

"Hmm, she was referred to the Coroner…," Logan recalls Catherine telling him, "…so if there was anything hinky the Forensic Pathologist would have found it."

"You would think so," Catherine agrees. "But there are

some drugs that don't show up in autopsy."

Almost choking on his bacon, Logan looks at Catherine as if she's gone mad. "Are you actually postulating that someone might have murdered her? Why on earth would anyone do that?"

Pursing her lips and frowning down as she cuts up her scrambled eggs on toast, Catherine can't actually think of a reason.

"I have no idea…," she finally admits, "…but I do know that it's happened before. And there was no good reason for it that time either!"

"When, and who did it?"

"She was convicted in 1993 and her name was Beverley Allitt," Catherine informs him. "She was a State Enrolled Nurse who appeared to suffer from Münchausen syndrome – attention seeking from being in on the care of her patients."

"Just…hold on a minute, I think I remember that case," Logan stops eating to concentrate. "Christ, yes, she was only about 24 or 25 and she was injecting her young charges with large doses of insulin."

Nodding, Catherine swallows a mouthful of breakfast then says, "She did that and other things. Even the doctors are not exactly sure how she carried out all of the attacks, but insulin did seem to be her drug of choice."

"It's a scary thought, isn't it, to think we trust our lives to so many people and it only takes one to end it on a whim," Logan muses.

"What a cheery thought," Mrs Baines gives Logan a lopsided smile with a raised brow. "Was there something in the paper?" she asks, nodding to the folded newspaper on the dining table.

"No, no, we were just discussing Beverley Allitt and Emma's aunt Izzy," Logan explains then realises he's only confused his housekeeper further. "Emma's aunt has just died in mysterious circumstances and Catherine has suggested that she might be the victim of murder," and he exaggerates the word to sound mysterious and scary.

Earning a kick to his shin for his trouble, Logan yelps and rubs it. "Hey, mind the legs, I've got a match this weekend," he grimaces.

"And you'll have a black eye to go with that sore shin if you keep ragging on me," Catherine scowls darkly.

"Now, now…," Mrs Baines restrains a grin valiantly, "…Catherine, tell me about Emma's aunt – what makes you think her death was anything more than unfortunate."

Glad to have someone take her seriously, Catherine goes into the doctor's remarks and the last notation in Isabelle's medical records.

"So you see, even they don't understand it," Catherine holds her hands up and shrugs her shoulders. "And it's not like it hasn't happened before!"

"Hmm, I don't want to start a scandal but it does seem a little odd," Mrs Baines shifts her focus to Logan. "I think it would certainly be worth a look, if Catherine can do so without raising the alarm."

Almost choking on her last mouthful of scrambled eggs on toast, Catherine turns a dark scowl on Mrs Baines.

"I do not raise alarms!" she states after getting her breath back. "I am extremely careful and brilliant at what I do!"

"And so modest," Logan grins teasingly.

"I'm just stating the facts. I can get in and out of any system without leaving a trace," she states unequivocally and with a determined lift of her chin.

"That may be so...," Mrs Baines interjects before an argument can ensue, "...but if you find anything suspicious you will need to inform the authorities. How will you explain where you got the information from?"

Not thrown for even a millisecond, Catherine shrugs and says, "I'll go to Frank Harper – he already knows what I do and manages to turn a blind eye. He'll make sure someone follows it up," she asserts confidently.

"And what about his partner, Shivers?" Logan asks, a

frown now darkening his lovely brown eyes. "He wasn't at all enamoured of your 'skills'," he emphasises quietly.

"He's a jerk. Personally I don't know what Emma sees in him," Catherine observes flatly. "Though, that is probably a moot point as they seem to have parted company."

"Oh, what a shame…," Mrs Baines exclaims, "…they seemed to make such a nice couple."

Catherine looks up at the housekeeper with a sceptical expression. "If you say so! But at least now she'll have her head back in the game. I swear she goes moony eyed every time that man walks in the damn room!"

Just then the front doorbell sounds and Mrs Baines goes off to answer it.

"Don't forget you have an appointment at our solicitors this morning," Logan reminds Catherine as they both stand and make their way into the hall.

"I know. And he's your solicitor, not 'ours'," she corrects him stubbornly.

"We are married, that makes him ours," Logan states just as stubbornly.

"Whatever! I hate doing all this formal stuff – why can't you just write something up and we'll sign it here?" Catherine suggests hopefully as they join Emma in the hallway.

"Because this is how business is done and it's best to get it done right!"

Frowning up at Logan, Catherine looks so put out that he half expects her to stamp her foot.

"What's going on?" Emma asks brightly.

"Ask him!" Catherine snaps, before she marches up the stairs to her new home office.

Quirking a brow at Logan, he just shakes his head and chuckles softly, leaving Emma to find out for herself.

"I'll ask again…," Emma stands, hands on hips, looking over at Catherine expectantly, "…what's going on? Were you not expecting me?"

"It had nothing to do with you," Catherine snaps, then looks up and frowns at Emma. "We have an appointment with Logan's solicitor. I hate those stuffy places; people look at you like you're less than subhuman and talk like they've got a hand full of plums in their damned mouths!"

Smiling, Emma realises that Catherine is being made to do something she doesn't want to.

A rarity, to say the least! No wonder she's all bent out of shape – it wasn't long ago that she pleased herself what she did; now she has a husband to answer to. That must chafe a bit!

"Hmm, so what's the appointment for?" Emma asks while rounding her desk to sit down.

"We're meeting Ben there. Logan thinks it's important to get the handover of Compusafe done legally." She didn't exactly roll her eyes, but Emma could imagine her doing it mentally anyway.

"Ben's a lucky so and so – it's not every day you get handed a lucrative business on a plate," Emma observes without the least bit of envy or bitterness.

"Well he did help me to build it up from next to nothing," Catherine explains. "In fact, if it hadn't been for Ben we wouldn't have made anywhere near as much money as we did. He charged the bloody earth for our services – I hate the money side of things!"

Hmm, so Ben has warned me. And while I have no problem with a bit of pro bono work I'll be making sure that our client's pay their bills!

"So what time are we meeting him – that is, if you need me to come along?" Emma asks uncertainly.

"Of course you're coming! I don't intend walking into that place on my own," Catherine's frown deepens at the thought.

"Not like you to be timid," Emma smiles.

"Timid be damned! I just don't want to go upsetting anyone and embarrassing Logan," Catherine states easily. "Not that he wouldn't deserve it – he could have made the papers up himself, I'm sure!"

"Err, no, he couldn't actually," Emma bravely corrects her boss. "It wouldn't be a very detailed legal document, and it needs to be to make the handover clear and official."

Narrowing her eyes, Catherine studies Emma hard. "Have you been talking to Logan?" she asks, though it sounds more like an accusation.

"Not at all," Emma shakes her head innocently. "But I imagine he said pretty much the same thing. It's standard practice to have a solicitor draw these types of contract up – they can protect your interests in ways we could hardly be expected to think of."

Relaxing back into her chair, Catherine continues to regard Emma suspiciously but not with any rancour.

"Hmm," Catherine grumbles and lowers her eyes to her laptop screen.

She's back into Isabelle's medical records and reading the last entry over again.

They may not have stated it openly, but even the doctors are suspicious. Otherwise, why would they have called a meeting to discuss her death and document it here in her notes?

But if I'm wrong about this I could just end up upsetting Emma for no good reason.

Shit! This friend stuff is complicated – and I thought

sisters were hard to weigh up! Dealing with Caroline and Adrianne is a breeze compared to this!

"What are you frowning over, now?" Emma asks close to Catherine's shoulder, making her jump.

"Jesus! Don't sneak up on me like that!" Catherine admonishes with a hand to her pounding heart

"I didn't sneak," Emma denies while reading Catherine's screen. "Are they my aunt's medical records?" she asks, astonished by the thought. "Why on earth are you reading her personal file?"

Becoming defensive, Catherine switches the screen on her laptop and scowls up at Emma.

"You shouldn't be reading over my shoulder – I could have been doing something private!"

"Instead you were poking your nose into my aunt's medical records," Emma states, hands on hips in an angry pose. "Why!?"

"None of your business," Catherine snaps unreasonably, unable to think of anything else to say that won't give her suspicions away.

"You…what…I don't believe it! You go through my aunt's confidential medical records, and who knows what else, then you have the cheek to tell me it's none of my business." Taking a deep breath, Emma tries and fails to calm down. "You tell me what's going on or I'm walking out and I won't be back, damn it!"

At the sound of raised voices, Logan takes the stairs two at a time to find out what's going on. "Ok, ladies, let's calm this down. What has happened?"

Both women glare at each other, neither of them forthcoming.

"Oookkk," Logan draws the tiny word out as he assesses the situation. "Then let me take a stab at guessing. Does it have something to do with your aunt's death?" he asks Emma, and sees by the incredulous look she gives him that he is right.

"What the hell is going on?" Emma demands, looking from Logan to Catherine and back again. "Why have you been looking into my aunt's medical records – and what do you mean by discussing my aunt's death?"

Knowing Catherine's lack of tact, Logan has to assume that she hasn't explained herself very well.

"It's just a theory that Catherine wanted to look into," he tells her quietly. "You expressed some concern over the circumstances of your aunt's death, and the concerns of the doctors caring for her – so Catherine took it on herself to dig a bit deeper," he sighs, his fingers rubbing at a growing tension headache.

"She wasn't prying – at least, she wasn't doing so out of malice or idle curiosity. Catherine was genuinely concerned and wanted to help if she could."

Listening to Logan has given Emma time to calm down, and now that she knows the reason for Catherine's meddling she is actually rather touched.

"You were trying to help," she tells Catherine, who is looking decidedly embarrassed. "And you didn't want me to know in case you didn't find anything," she guesses, and sees Catherine give a single nod of affirmation.

"I didn't want to raise your hopes or make any assumptions until I'd had time to verify my findings," Catherine admits sheepishly.

"Ok." Emma looks at the floor, thinking things through then asks, "Who's for coffee?"

Catherine looks blankly at Logan as Emma moves across the room to the kettle and switches it on. But he just smiles.

"What do you think to your new office?" he asks conversationally, relaxing now that the storm has passed.

"It's really great," Emma answers agreeably as she gathers mugs together and spoons coffee into them. "Will we be able to replicate this setup when we move to Lakelands?"

"This and more," Logan tells her. "The room we've allocated is twice the size of this one, so you'll have even more room to move and organise yourselves."

"So if I want to send her to Coventry…," Emma jabs a thumb in Catherine's direction, "…I can just work at the opposite end of the room?"

"You can work on the other side of Timbuktu for all I care," Catherine snaps, but there is no venom in her voice now.

Logan takes the mug of coffee that Emma hands him and watches cautiously as she takes Catherine's coffee to her.

"You pissed me off, but I know you meant well," Emma states, her frown breaking into a smile. "Just come clean with me another time. Though I hope to God no one else in my family dies in suspicious circumstances!"

"Good coffee," Catherine states, holding her mug out after taking a sip. And Emma knows that's the closest she's going to get to an apology.

"Glad you like it. Now tell me what you've found out so far."

Logan turns and leaves unnoticed, sure now that the two women are back on level ground.

She's got spine, I'll give Emma that much. I'm not sure I'd like to be the one working so closely with Catherine — she can be a tigress when her claws come out. Then you'd better be out of arms reach!

Chuckling, Logan reassures Mrs Baines that the girls haven't come to blows.

Catherine turns her attention back to her laptop and switches the screen back to show Isabelle's medical records.

"See here…," Catherine points out the last entry made by her aunt's medical team, "…they had a powwow to discuss Isabelle's unexpected death. They even state that in her notes, right here," Catherine points to the screen at the appropriate paragraph.

"Yes, I see," Emma agrees. "But what can we get from this? I mean, they don't actually speculate about the cause of death — they just acknowledge that it was unexpected."

"Not right here they don't," Catherine agrees. "But look at this," she tells Emma, scrolling further down the page to another section. "They discussed her electrolyte balance and the fact that her potassium level was on the high side." Then Catherine explains the relevance of this as Emma looks confused. "Potassium affects cardiac function; too high or too low it can cause arrhythmias and the like, and can even lead to a heart attack."

Looking taken aback, Emma asks, "How do you know that stuff?"

Shrugging her shoulders, Catherine replies, "I read a lot."

"You read medical books?"

"I read a lot of stuff," Catherine tells her flatly.

Straightening, Emma has to pace to gather her chaotic thoughts.

Can this even be real? Could someone have deliberately taken aunt Izzy's life? Damn it, it sounds plausible and crazy at the same time. How would we even look into something like this, never mind have a hope of proving anything!

"We can do this," Catherine assures her, as if Emma had spoken her thoughts aloud. "One way or the other, we'll either prove she was murdered – in which case there could be other victims – or we'll lay all of the concerns to rest and you can move on."

Watching her new colleague and friend with baited breath, Catherine can see the struggle going on inside Emma.

On the one hand she wants to know the truth, but the thought that her aunt has been murdered is hard to bear.

I could just bury my head in the sand and let it all go away – but that's the coward's way out. And aunt Izzy deserves better than that!

"Ok…where do we start?"

Heaving a sigh of relief, Catherine sends the medical notes to the printer so that they have a copy to refer back to without having to constantly hack into the records.

"I suggest we start looking for other possible victims," Catherine suggests. "It's a mixed sex ward – I'll take the women and you take the men. We'll go back over the last 12 months and see what we come up with."

For just a moment, Emma hesitates, then moves to her laptop with grim determination in her eyes.

So, this is to be our first case. I just hope I can handle what we find, but find it we will if there's anything amiss. I owe you that much, aunt Izzy – we'll find out if someone hurt you, you can count on that!

CHAPTER THREE

"I swear, if I get any bigger I'll pop," Caroline groans as she all but rolls out of bed.

But Travis knows she is happy with her pregnancy and looking forward to the girls' arrival as much as he.

"You are always beautiful," he tells her, pulling her into his arms. "And your sister is just as big as you – in fact, as ungallant as it sounds, I'd say Catherine might be a touch bigger."

Tilting her face up to kiss him, Caroline knows her husband is just trying to make her feel better. "You say the sweetest things, even if they aren't true," she chuckles softly.

Then she frowns and looks at Travis with troubled eyes.

"What is it?" he asks, seeing a cloud pass over her lovely face.

"I don't know...I...I just thought of Catherine and, I know this is going to sound crazy, but I felt really sad," she tells him, her sister's face still clear in her mind's eye.

Guiding her to a nearby settee, Travis sits beside Caroline and studies her carefully.

"You're not feeling ill, or faint?" he asks, his deep voice gentle with concern.

Putting a hand over his, Caroline assures him that all is well, in her world at least.

"But I think something is wrong with Catherine," she tells him, still not able to shake the feeling. "And you don't need to tell me how crazy I sound, but...could we go visit? Just for a while, it would put my mind at ease."

When they arrive at Catherine and Logan's house, Caroline takes Travis's arm to pull him to a stop. "I feel it stronger, now," she tells him. "Travis, I'm scared."

Putting an arm across her shoulders, he pulls her to him and steers her to the front door.

"Well we won't find anything out standing out here," he chides softly.

Only moments later, Mrs Baines answers the door and welcomes them inside.

"Everyone seems to be working," she tells them with a pleasant grin. "Catherine and Emma are upstairs in their new office and Logan actually went in to work this morning. Though he's due back any time now," the housekeeper informs them. "He doesn't like to leave Catherine for long."

"Is it alright if we go up?" Caroline asks.

"Of course. Of course. I'll bring you all up some tea and coffee in just a few minutes," Mrs Baines smiles, then goes back into her kitchen.

"Stop worrying...," Travis tells Caroline as he walks beside her up the stairs, "...you probably only thought about your sister because I mentioned her."

Travis has told her this a number of times on the way over, but it still isn't making Caroline feel any better.

"You're probably right...," she says again, "...but I'll believe it more when I've seen Catherine for myself."

Walking along a short landing, they hear a muted conversation and make their way towards the sound of voices.

Knocking first, Travis opens the door and ushers Caroline inside.

"Hey sis, what are you doing here?" Catherine smiles, her troubles falling away instantly at the sight of her twin.

"Are you alright?" Caroline asks, crossing the room and ignoring her sister's question.

"I'm fine, why?"

Caroline heaves a heavy sigh, then sits down opposite

Catherine, grateful to take the weight off her feet.

Rubbing a hand over her moist eyes, she tries to rid herself of the peculiar sadness that is still enveloping her.

"I thought of you and I felt so sad," she tries to explain. Then inexplicably tears start to fall uncontrollably. "And I still feel really sad – but it doesn't feel like it's me, it feels like I'm feeling your sadness."

Emma discreetly leaves the room, closing the door behind her.

"Have you had this before?" Catherine asks.

At first, Caroline shakes her head, then stops and looks at Catherine with narrowed eyes.

"Yes, I think I have – though I wouldn't have known it was your sadness I was experiencing," she admits uncertainly.

With raised brows, Catherine leans forward on her desk regarding her twin with dubious eyes.

"I can see you don't believe me," Caroline states, using the handkerchief her husband has given her. "And I know it sounds completely barmy – but I'm telling you, it wasn't my sadness...it was yours."

Getting up, Catherine begins to pace the room, thinking back on her thoughts and feelings during the morning.

"How long ago did this happen? This feeling of sadness," she clarifies.

"About an hour ago," Caroline states, looking up at Travis for confirmation.

"Yes, that sounds about right," he nods.

Looking at her watch, Catherine works backwards to remember what she was doing and crossing back to her laptop, begins to study it.

"That was when I found our second possible victim," she murmurs quietly.

A 51 year old single mother of three children, the youngest being just 10 – all she'd gone in for was to have her shattered leg pinned back together after surviving a car accident with no other injuries. And then she'd died – no warning symptoms, no indication at all that anything was amiss. Just like Isabelle!

"I don't understand...are you working a case already? I didn't think you were up and running yet?" Caroline asks, looking confused.

"We aren't. At least, not officially," Catherine tells her, then explains about Emma's aunt and the theory they're working.

"And you think that poor woman was another victim? No wonder you were so sad," Caroline sighs, drying her cheeks of the last of her errant tears.

"And you really felt that?" Catherine asks incredulous.

"Yes, I was so sure, it was almost physical, the

connection I felt with you," Caroline explains, not really understanding the concept herself.

"I've heard of twins, even non-identical twins, having this kind of link," Travis interjects. "I suppose the fact that you are identical twins, formed from the same DNA, might make that link even stronger."

"Maybe it's only just started to gain strength as we've grown closer," Catherine speculates. "And we live closer now than before."

"I don't think distance is a factor," Travis tells them. "I've heard of cases where one twin felt the other twin's pain on the other side of the world. Or some have been known to feel the connection sever completely when the other twin died."

The two women just look at each other, words not necessary to convey how distraught each felt at the idea of losing the other.

"Maybe that explains my sudden mood swings," Catherine smiles to lift the mood.

Hesitantly, Caroline tells Catherine of another time she is sure that she felt her sister's pain. "I did some checking a couple of weeks ago...," she begins cautiously, "...and I was in counselling at school at the same time as you went into psychiatric care."

Getting to her feet, it is Caroline's turn to pace the

office. "I know it sounds crazy, but I crashed and burned for no good reason. I just felt like my world had turned on its head and I was alone. So alone..."

"Don't!" Catherine moves to her sister and wraps an arm around her shoulders, hugging as best as two women can who are both 33 weeks pregnant with twins. "You're not alone and never will be. We found each other, and we found Adrianne, nothing will separate us again."

"And dad...?"

Nodding, Catherine smiles, "And dad, too."

"Ok, I feel better now that I know you're ok," Caroline smiles at her sister. "I'll leave you to your work now. And I'll tell Emma the coast is clear to come back up."

"Thanks." Moving to Travis, Catherine gives him a brief hug too. She still isn't comfortable with her feelings, and showing them is difficult for Catherine. "Take care of my sister."

"Always my pleasure," Travis tells her, dropping a kiss on Catherine's head.

You're so like Logan. Maybe that's a twin thing too – we both love the same kind of men.

When Emma comes back into the office, Catherine explains why Caroline was so upset.

"I guess that's something you're going to have to get used to," Emma speculates with a raised brow. "But at least now you know where those unexpected emotions are coming from – it must have been strange to suddenly go from happy to sad or frightened without knowing why!"

Frowning, Catherine leans back in her chair and looks up at Emma, who is standing in front of her desk.

"I've always known I'm different...strange and...unpredictable," she eventually decides. "Maybe this really does explain some of that."

"Ha!" Emma laughs good humouredly. "That's just an excuse - admit it, you're just plain strange and taciturn!"

"And I'm still your boss, damn it!" Catherine throws a small desk rubber at her colleague and chuckles when Emma twists her body out of the way.

Then Logan is at the door, looking at Catherine with a frown and shaking his head in despair, tapping his wrist watch.

"Oh shit!" Catherine jumps to her feet and then looks horrified. "You did it again! You made me swear in front of the children. Damn it Logan!"

"If you would just remember your appointments I wouldn't have to come and remind you," he tells her with an amused smile.

"What appointment?" Emma asks.

"I told you, we have to meet Ben at Logan's solicitors,"

Catherine tells her, ignoring her husband's frown at her reference to 'Logan's' solicitor.

Going to move past him, Catherine is mortified when he pulls her into his arms and kisses her in front of Emma.

"Logan!"

"What, Emma knows we kiss," Logan laughs at Catherine's discomfort. "I bet she knows we do other things too," he adds, enjoying her embarrassment.

Giving him a hard thump to his arm, Catherine pushes past and says, "Men!" then listens to her husband and Emma laughing as she quickly makes her way downstairs.

Ben is already at the solicitor's office by the time they arrive and he greets them warmly.

"Hey, gorgeous," he grins, giving Catherine a brief hug. "How are you doing?" he asks Emma as he looks over Catherine's shoulder.

"I'm fine," Emma assures him.

"Well, let's get this thing done," Catherine tells no one in particular, and strides over to the reception desk. "Catherine Colson-Sayers to see Mr Willard."

"I'll just let him know you're here," the young woman smiles pleasantly. "Would you like to take a seat?"

Catherine just frowns and remains standing at the desk, her intimidation tactics getting just the response she'd anticipated.

Instead of dealing with anything else, the receptionist immediately picks up the telephone and rings through to Mr Willard and does indeed let him know that his clients have arrived.

Moments later, Douglas Willard comes to the door and invites the small group through to his office.

Shaking their hands, he indicates the seats he has set out and rounds his desk to retake his own.

"Good to see you, Catherine," Douglas smiles. "Haven't seen you for a while, how are you keeping?"

"I'm fine, thank you," she smiles shyly.

"Good. Good," he smiles back.

Opening a manila folder on his desk, Douglas leafs through the papers inside it and pulls a couple of them forward.

"I've drawn up this contract, as your husband asked me to do on your behalf...," Douglas again smiles over at Catherine, "...and, if you are absolutely sure that you wish to proceed, we can officially sign over the ownership of Compusafe to Mr Benjamin Sharman," and he turns his smile on Ben, whose beaming smile could light up all of London!

"Ok, just show me where to sign," Catherine tells the solicitor, eager to get the job done and get out of there. *It's places like this that give me the willies!*

With a brief explanation of exactly what he is asking them to sign, the solicitor turns pages and points to where first Catherine and then Ben need to add their signatures.

Standing, he hands one copy of the contract to Catherine and the other to a very happy Ben.

Shaking hands, Douglas eyes Ben speculatively. No doubt wondering what he's done to earn this enormity of a gift from his former boss. But it isn't his place to question.

Retaking his seat, Douglas takes out another manila file and takes out more papers.

"Now, shall we get down to the second order of business?" Douglas smiles at Catherine, then confuses Emma when he turns the same smile to include her.

"This contract spells out the formalities of setting up your new business," he tells both women, causing Emma's frown to deepen. "CCS Investigations will officially be formed on this date once your signatures are added to this partnership agreement."

Turning to Catherine, Emma gasps, "What?!"

Surprised by Emma's reaction, Catherine goes on the defensive. "Well, hell, I just thought it would save time! I mean, the last time I did this I ended up making Ben a partner anyway — so I just thought we might as well start as we mean to go on. What's so damned wrong with that?!"

"I...don't know what to say," Emma gapes at Catherine.

When Catherine remains silent and sullen, Douglas decides to step in.

"Catherine will retain a controlling interest as she is providing the start up capital and the business premises, as well as covering the cost of all related bills," he explains, mainly for Emma's benefit as Catherine has already been apprised of the details of the contract.

"Your share of the partnership will be 40%, a very generous arrangement," Douglas smiles at Emma, then manages to catch Catherine's eye.

"Are we ready to sign?" he asks with a raised brow.

"Catherine, I never dreamed this is what you intended," Emma tells her new boss quietly. "I can't thank you enough for this opportunity."

Realising that she has completely misread the situation, Catherine turns a less stern frown to her new partner. "So, you're not mad?" she asks, still not sure of Emma's mood.

"No I'm not mad," Emma shakes her head in exasperation. "I was just shocked and a little thrown is all." Then Emma cracks a smile and wags a finger at Catherine, "Just because you've got controlling interest, don't expect me to cow-tow to your every whim. If I disagree with you I intend to tell you so – so if that doesn't suit..."

"That suits me fine," Catherine continues to frown, then breaks out into a beautiful smile. "Yes, that suits me just fine."

CHAPTER FOUR

When Emma pulls up on Catherine's drive, she turns off the ignition then turns in her seat to face Catherine.

"I feel sort of...dazed," Emma confesses. "This morning I turned up for work excited for a new challenge. And now..."

"Now you not only have a new challenge you have new responsibilities," Catherine states, matter of fact. "This agency won't grow all by itself – we will need to be focused and hardworking."

"Absolutely," Emma agrees. "But I was thinking more of the 'Oh my God, I can't believe I'm a partner in my own business' kind of dazed!"

Heaving herself out of the car, Catherine waddles to the front door with Emma scooting after her.

Putting her key in the lock, Catherine looks back at Emma and allows herself a smile.

"I suppose it is kind of monumental when you think about it," she tells Emma, then pushes the door open and walks through to the kitchen. "Mrs B, do we have any champagne?"

Raising a brow, the housekeeper goes to the cold room where Logan keeps his wine and brings back a bottle of champagne.

"Are you celebrating something" Mrs Baines asks when she sees Catherine and Emma grinning at each other.

"We most certainly are," Emma giggles lightly. "This mad woman just signed away a multimillion pound company on the one hand and gave me a 40% partnership in our new venture with the other!"

"Did I hear you say we're celebrating?" Logan asks as he comes into the kitchen.

"It seems we are," Mrs Baines chuckles, taking champagne flutes out of a nearby cupboard.

Catherine looks crestfallen. "Surely I can have half a glass," she bemoans on seeing only three glasses.

"Well, of course you can dear," Mrs Baines smiles. "Won't do you or the baby a bit of harm."

Frowning, Catherine watches the housekeeper pour the drinks then hand them out.

"Where's yours?" she asks the housekeeper bluntly.

Waving it off, Mrs Baines says," I wouldn't presume. This is your special celebration."

But Catherine just crosses to the cupboard and takes out another glass.

"Come on, fill her up," she tells Mrs Baines, and watches the housekeeper smile.

"Well, thank you very much," she tells them, then lifts her glass and says, "Congratulations – may your new venture be successful in every way!"

"Cheers," Logan toasts, and all four of them chink their glasses together.

Less than an hour later, all thoughts of champagne and celebrations are forgotten.

"I think I've found another possible," Emma frowns at her computer screen. "George Ritter, 53, admitted with multiple fractures to his lower leg – apparently caused by a bad tackle during a game of football."

"What the hell was he doing playing football at 53?" Catherine asks inanely, crossing the room to look at Emma's laptop.

"He was a father of two grown children, widowed young and was on the road to discharge, just like the others," Emma looks up at Catherine.

"I agree, he's another possible. Print out his details and we'll add him to the board."

"Catherine, if we're right about even just these three cases, shouldn't we tell someone?"

If I go to Harper with this it will no doubt mean Shivers getting in on the act and he's a pain in the arse! But Emma's right, we need to tell someone – maybe I could talk to Harper on his own, make it a friendly chat...

"I'll call Frank Harper, ask him to meet me for lunch and a friendly chat," Catherine nods, agreeing with her own thoughts. "I don't want Shivers involved until we know a lot more. But Frank...he's more open minded."

"So you're asking me to keep quiet?" Emma clarifies with a raised brow.

"Be honest, would you want Shivers looking over your shoulder while you hack into medical records?" Catherine asks bluntly.

Looking more than a little uncomfortable at the thought, Emma shakes her head.

"Right then, we talk to Frank and get his opinion. He might have tips on where to look for evidence and how to pin down the perpetrator...if there is one," she adds when Emma pales.

"It's looking likely," Emma sits back in her seat looking over at Catherine. "I don't like to think that aunt Izzy was murdered, but I wouldn't want the killer to get away with it just because I'm too yellow to face facts."

"You are anything but yellow," Catherine states firmly. "I'd be just as reluctant to accept that someone I loved had been murdered in this way, when they were putting all their trust in someone that should have been helping them. But I'd be determined to track down the culprit and get them off the streets."

With a sympathetic smile, Catherine moves back to her desk and retakes her seat.

"We can't let this person kill someone else's aunt or father or mother or daughter – we need to stop this as fast as we can." Then Catherine grimaces, "Even if it means working with that stiff-neck you're seeing, Sloane Shivers!" and she gives a full body shiver for dramatic effect causing Emma to chuckle.

"He's not so bad outside of work," she explains. "Sloane just doesn't like to get his lines blurred – it kinda throws him off balance. But he can be funny when he's off duty. He's usually kind and considerate-"

"When he's not being an arsehole," Catherine interjects.

Taking a deep breath, Emma lets it out slowly, calming her instinct to go back at Catherine.

"Sloane can be..."

"A dickhead," Catherine puts in before Emma can finish.

"Will you stop! I really like the man you're ragging on, so a little restraint in the name calling department wouldn't go amiss," Emma growls out, her voice becoming firm and loud.

"Gotcha!" Catherine laughs, happy that her plan to distract Emma's thought's away from her useless guilt has worked.

"You...you..." Emma takes another deep breath and again lets it out slowly. "You were just winding me up – why?"

"Because you rise to it so well," Catherine chuckles. "And because you're the only person I know who doesn't balk at a good shouting match – you'll keep me on my toes."

Bemused and a little uncertain, Emma just shakes her head and goes back to the job in hand.

"It'll be a doctor or a nurse, right – the person who's doing this?" Emma muses out loud. "I mean, they are the ones with access to the drugs so it's bound to be one of them, right?"

When Emma looks over at Catherine she is surprised to see her shake her head. "What if the perp brought the drugs in from home? What if they are diabetic and used some of their own insulin to bump off a patient or two?"

Emma's jaw drops open, "But that could mean any

number of people! Think of all the relatives that visit — we'll never track them all down!"

But again, Catherine shakes her head. "No, relatives are not in the running. These murders have taken place over time — they would have no reason to be there after their relative is discharged or dies. But cleaners, porters, nursing assistants, and God knows who else, do have reasons for being there."

"Jesus! That's still a lot of people to look at," Emma sighs.

"It is, but we'll stick with the medics and nurses to begin with," Catherine suggests. "They are the more likely candidates and we may get lucky. We'll only spread out to the other staff if we can't find any connections."

"What about Frank, are you going to give him a call?"

"On it," Catherine states, picking up her mobile and flicking through her contacts.

"Damn it — straight to voice mail!" Catherine glares at the phone then tries it again, when it goes to voice mail for a second time she leaves a terse message.

"Hey, Frank, Catherine Colson-Sayers here, give me a call when you get this."

Emma chuckles softly. "Well that was short and to the point."

"Agh, I hate leaving messages," Catherine scowls at

her mobile. "Why can't people just answer their damned phones?!"

"Could be he's in a meeting," Emma offers. "Or grilling a suspected murderer, trying to break him down and get him to confess," she adds in a mysterious sounding voice that has Catherine laughing.

"God, you're so full of it," Catherine tells her not unkindly. "But I suppose your enthusiasm for all things 'murder and mystery' are good traits to have in this business."

Just then, Catherine's mobile rings and she answers it quickly when she see's Franks ID.

"Hi," she greets him.

"Sorry I missed your call," Frank apologises. "I was in with the 'brass'."

Catherine can hear the undertone in his voice and guesses that it wasn't a good meeting.

"Are you in trouble?" she asks, concerned.

"Not exactly, they're after some good PR and want us to perform like dancing monkeys to get it," Frank tells her, a scathing note in his voice now. "If they hadn't been stuck behind their desks for so long, they'd have a better idea of what 'good PR' really is, as far as everyday people are concerned."

"You mean upping the arrest and conviction rates?" Catherine suggests.

"I do indeed. That's what the everyday citizen cares about," Frank grumbles, then she hears the smile return to his voice. "Well now, that's my little moan for the day over with – how may I help you, my dear?"

Catherine smiles at his good natured dismissal of his own problems and his willingness to hear about hers.

"How about I buy you lunch?" she asks brightly.

"You want to buy me lunch?" he asks inanely.

"I do indeed...," she confirms, "...then I can pick your brains about a case we're looking into. Are you up for it?"

Without hesitation, Frank agrees.

"Ok, how about The Coffee Pot café, I can be there in half an hour?" she tells him brightly.

Ending the call, Catherine looks over at her partner in crime, "That's me sorted for lunch – what are you planning to do? Mrs B would happily prepare you something."

"No, no. I wouldn't dream of imposing," Emma declines quickly. "I brought my lunch with me, so I'm set."

"Ok, if you're sure?"

"You go and do what you need to and I'll chill right here for half an hour."

Because Logan doesn't like her driving now that she is so far along with the twins, Catherine allows him to call a taxi for her.

"I'm sure I can still fit behind the wheel," she complains, though not very convincingly.

"I'm sure you could," Logan agrees, bending to give her a kiss. "But I won't worry half as much if I know you are being driven. In fact, why don't you employ a secretary come driver – she'd be at your beck and call whenever you want to go anywhere?"

Grimacing up at him, Catherine secretly thinks it might be a good idea. But she doesn't like the idea of interviewing people for the job.

"I'll think about it."

"Good, then I'll think about not being jealous of you taking another man out to lunch," he tells her, surprising Catherine no end.

"Are you nuts!" she gapes at him, not sure if Logan is being serious or not.

"Pregnant or not, you are a beautiful woman with an intriguing mind. I'm sure someone like Frank Harper would find you a very attractive prospect," Logan smiles.

Deciding that he can't be being serious, Catherine gives him a thump to his upper arm.

"You moron – you had me going there for a minute!"

But just as Catherine is about to turn and leave, Logan gently takes hold of her arm.

"I know you don't see yourself as others do – as men

do – but I guard what's mine, Catherine, make no mistake about that."

Then Logan catches her to him and kisses her until her mind whirls and her heart beats wildly beneath her heaving breasts.

"I love you, Catherine," his brown eyes are hot and melting. "I never joke about us."

Then he is gone, leaving Catherine shaken and her body thoroughly stirred.

What the hell! I look like a beached whale and he thinks a man like Frank would find me attractive? Jesus...what is that man on!

When her taxi pulls up outside of The Coffee Pot café, Catherine pays the fare and looks around for Inspector Frank Harper.

"Catherine!"

Hearing her name called, she turns in the hailer's direction to see Frank Harper jogging up to her.

"Sorry, got held up at the station," he apologises as he comes along side her. "You look radiant – pregnancy suits you, my dear."

Blushing, Catherine looks at him warily.

Damn you, Logan, for putting stupid ideas in my head! Now I'll be thinking all sorts of things when I need to concentrate on the case!

"Shall we go in?" Frank asks, holding the door open when Catherine hesitates.

"Sure, let's get something to eat – I'm starving," she tells him, then realises that she actually is.

After ordering their meals, Frank turns to Catherine with curiosity in his eyes.

"So, what's this about...," he asks, his eyes narrowed, "...I rarely get asked out to lunch by a beautiful woman so I have to guess it's my police skills you're after?"

Taking a sip of her juice, Catherine almost chokes on it before she can answer him.

"Are you alright, my dear?" he asks, rising to pat her back.

"Just swallowed the wrong way," she excuses, promising herself to give Logan some payback when she gets home. "I'm ok – and yes, it is your police skills I want to utilise."

"Fire away, this sounds intriguing."

Jesus, isn't that what Logan said – he'll find you intriguing, or some such shit!

Giving herself a mental shake, Catherine brings her thoughts back to the matter in hand.

"Emma and I, you know that we're starting up our own investigations agency," she tells him, watching while he nods. "Well, we're working our first case and it's personal."

"Personal?" he frowns. "If there's a problem I can help you with, Catherine, you know you only have to ask."

"It's Emma, I know she won't mind me telling you, her aunt has just died in mysterious circumstances," she explains. "According to the doctors it was entirely unexpected. She had surgery on a hip that got fractured in a fall, and she was making a good recovery – was expected to be discharged in a couple of days."

Catherine frowns and sighs, taking another sip of her juice. "I started digging around..."

"As you do," Frank chuckles softly.

"As I do," she echoes, then her expression becomes dark with concern. "I think we found more victims."

Now it's Frank's turn to choke on his tea. "Victims! You honestly think Emma's aunt was murdered?"

"I do," she nods. "And I think we'll find even more victims if we keep looking."

The waitress comes to their booth and places their lunch in front of them. Only when she's gone does their conversation continue.

"Catherine, this is a serious accusation to make," Frank warns her, his voice low and dire. "If word of this gets out, and is proved to be unfounded, you could be charged with slander and brought up in the courts yourself!"

"What are you saying — that I should drop it?" she asks, her eyes narrowed and assessing.

"I don't think it would make a difference if I were — you'd continue no matter what," he tells her, his lips pursed while he shakes his head at her. "This isn't like your mother — you can't just go digging around in hospital business, trying to pin murder on them!"

Sitting back in her seat, Catherine has lost her appetite. "I thought you, of all people, would be on my side. Just goes to show!"

Sliding along the seat, Catherine makes to get up, but finds her hand being held by Frank across the table.

"I'm sorry, my dear. Please don't go like this," he tells her, his eyes pleading with her to stay. "It isn't that I don't want to help, but I need to caution you about what you are undertaking."

Sliding back into her seat, Catherine takes another sip of juice while regarding him steadily.

"I don't think you quite grasp the enormity of what you've started," Frank tells her in hushed tones. "And I'm not saying that you have to stop — just be extremely careful!"

Realising that she has probably overreacted, Catherine nods and gives him a glimpse of a smile.

"I suppose I just didn't expect you to be the one on my

back," she tells him honestly. "It was Shivers I thought would give us the hassle."

Chuckling softly, Frank nods his agreement. "Hmm, and I'm sure he will if he ends up coming in on this. But I won't be apprising him of the situation unless we find solid evidence of wrong doing."

"So you're willing to help?" she eyes him speculatively.

"Of course. But let's not discuss it any further here. I'll call round to the house later this evening, if that's alright with you?" Frank asks.

"No problem. How does between 6 and 7 sound...," Catherine asks quietly, "...that way we can discuss everything without upsetting Emma. She'll have gone home by then."

<u>CHAPTER FIVE</u>

The Orthopaedics ward is buzzing. They've had so many admissions that Helen's head is spinning.

And the discharges are just as bad. The paperwork is ridiculous and those bossy nurses think they're the only ones that have to do any.

Well, ours might be on computer but we still have to take the time to do it all. Every patient has to be clerked in, admitted on the computer system and demographics labels printed off, and then we have to transfer them to other wards on the same system – or do a complete discharge if they've gone home directly from us.

Either way, we have our own jobs to do!

"Helen, we need help to clean a bed station," Staff Nurse Barbara Davies stops beside the Health Care Assistant (HCA) who is sat working on a computer.

"Ok. Just give me a sec' to finish this and I'll be right on it," Helen smiles up. *Another job we end up doing that is the nurse's responsibility! They treat us like domestics half the time – until they want to go for a break. Then we're good enough to keep an eye on the patients so that they can go out back for tea and coffee.*

Getting a mop and bucket and making up some Chlorclean, Helen uses it to wipe down all the surfaces and equipment that occupy the now empty bed-space.

And just look at that – more drugs left in the bedside locker that should have gone home with the patient and...ah, yes, Mrs Greaves was diabetic, they've left her insulin in here too.

Clearing out the drug locker, Helen wipes it clean, inside and out, then takes the medication to the clinical area and places them in a patient's own drugs bag with a name label attached to it, then passes it off to the nurse who'd been looking after that patient.

Sloppy! Very sloppy!

Within half an hour another patient is occupying that same bed-space and Helen is back on the computer to admit them on the system.

Later that afternoon, after the drug round is finished, the lights are dimmed and the patients encouraged to have a rest.

This is the period that Helen loves. She makes the time to chat with the patients, seeing to their comfort and maybe getting them a hot drink if they fancy one.

She is known for her compassion.

"How are you, Mr Weston – is the pain any better today?" she asks, taking a seat next to his bed.

"Not too bad," Mr Weston smiles over at his favourite nurse. "I don't suppose we can expect to be pain free after a hip replacement," he tells her stoically.

Although Helen isn't a qualified nurse, most of the patients refer to her as 'nurse'. And she enjoys the title that she hasn't earned.

"If you let us know, we can usually give you something to ease it," she assures him. "But if you don't speak up, how will we know?"

Patting her hand, the old gentleman in bed six gives her a smile before his eyes drift closed and he falls asleep.

It isn't right! They sit chatting and stand in corners where they think no one knows they're sneakily talking or texting on their damn mobiles, when what they should be doing is looking after their patients!

Stroking his hand, Helen watches as he cringes in his sleep – the pain causing him discomfort even as he dreams.

Don't you worry, I won't leave you to suffer like this.

You're such a lovely man, and they just leave you to suffer because you're too nice to speak up for yourself.

I've seen them; they haven't got five minutes to spend with the likes of you. You don't make a fuss so they leave you alone – alone and in pain!

Helen looks around, sees the nurses going about their business, or standing together chatting, and her rage quietly grows.

If you were a patient I'll bet you'd be crying out for pain relief and you wouldn't accept 'sorry, it isn't time for the drug round yet' as an excuse for not getting any!

Damned prima-donna's! And the doctors are no better – they write them up for Paracetamol and expect it to cure all ill!

I swear, if it weren't for me these poor people would be left to suffer. But I won't let that happen.

Fingering the Insulin vial in her pocket, Helen makes her way down the ward and to the treatment room, where the needles and syringes are kept and drugs are drawn up.

When Inspector Frank Harper arrives at Catherine and Logan's house he is in possession of a few more facts.

Accepting the mug of coffee that Catherine offers him, Frank takes a seat in the sitting room and is surprised to see Emma.

She must have got wind of my visit and insisted on staying. Still, if she's going to be working this case she might as well be up to date on everything.

Carefully, Frank begins to share his findings.

"I spoke to a trusted friend of mine, a Forensic Pathologist, strictly off the record and only giving the barest details of what we're looking into," Frank tells them quietly. "He told me that he, too, has noticed more of these cases coming across his table."

"Has he reported his suspicions?" Catherine asks, hoping that someone in authority is, even now, looking into the situation.

"No...," Frank shakes his head, "...for the very same reasons that I gave you, Catherine. This is an extremely sensitive area – if he, or you, were to voice those concerns outside of this group all hell would ensue."

"But we can't let it continue," Emma stands abruptly, clearly upset by the idea of doing nothing. "Surely, now that you know your Pathologist friend has his own suspicions, you can take this investigation up formally!"

But Frank sadly shakes his head. "I'm sorry, my dear...without evidence of wrongdoing my Chief wouldn't touch this with a barge-pole."

"It's a powder-keg alright," Logan agrees.

Looking to each person in turn, Emma's tear filled

eyes turn hot and angry. "So we just let whoever it is, continue to murder people just because it might cause a public outcry?"

"I will, of course, continue to look into this matter on the QT," Frank assures her. "But I can't open an official investigation until we have some evidence. It would send people into a panic – you must see that."

Reluctantly, unable to speak because of the threatening tears, Emma nods her agreement.

"That doesn't mean we stop looking," Catherine assures her. "We'll keep digging until we find the evidence Frank needs, then it will be full steam ahead – right Frank?"

"Right," he agrees firmly. "And you girls are so good at what you do; you're bound to find something that I can use."

"Do you want to take a look at the boards we've started?" Catherine asks.

"That's a good idea – it will help me to follow what you've found already and give me a place to continue looking," Frank replies, standing to make his way to their home office.

When he looks at the setup of their office, Frank nods in approval. "This is a great space," he commends.

Then he turns to the boards they have started and the suspected victims.

"Five," he gasps in surprise. "You've already found five?"

"Yes," Catherine confirms. "We looked back over the last 12 months to start with, then decided to go back another 12."

Stepping forward, Catherine takes him through the cases. "These latest two are only 3 months apart, yet the other three are around 5 and 6 months apart," she explains.

"We've gone through their medical records and can't see any reason for their deaths – or any reason they've been singled out," Catherine tells Frank with a frown. "They are all Orthopaedic patients, and all were in for some kind of surgery, but that's the extent of their connection. As far as we can see, anyway," Catherine adds.

Taking a dry-wipe pen, Frank writes on the whiteboard. "All over the age of 50," he tells them as he writes. "That might be an important factor, or it might not. But it's worth making a note of anything like that, even if you have to alter it later."

"Ok," Catherine nods.

Do they all have spouses – or do they live alone?" Frank asks.

"Bloody hell!" Catherine snaps, then realises that

she's just sworn. "Crap!" she whispers, looking over at Logan who just smiles. "We just looked at those who had family and those who didn't," She tells him.

"Obviously Emma's aunt had family, but she also lived alone – we'll need to look at the others to see what their living arrangements were," she concedes.

"Don't start beating yourselves up over this," Frank smiles reassuringly. "I've had years of doing these things, you'll soon get the knack of what to look for."

Emma and Catherine start flipping through the background notes on each subject and come up with the surprising conclusion that they all live alone – although obviously, the woman with the 3 children wasn't entirely alone. But there was no other adult living in the house.

"You think that's part of the criteria the murderer has for taking them out?" Catherine asks, still unhappy that she didn't think to look for that connection.

"It looks like it could be," Frank tells them as he writes that fact under the 'over 50' comment on the board.

"But that could change, right?" Logan asks. "I mean, don't these people sometimes escalate and change their original pattern of behaviour?"

Nodding, Frank turns to Logan. "Yes, that's why it's important to keep an eye on the pattern as it unfolds." Pointing at the board, Frank makes a supposition," Just the two facts that we have listed here could mean that the murderer is targeting the elderly and lonely – perhaps relating it back to something that happened to a relative in their own lives. Someone who, for some reason, they either murdered or wanted to murder."

"You mean, it could be someone who treated the murderer badly and now they're paying every like person back for it?" Emma asks, troubled to think her kind and bubbly aunt had been punished for someone else's crime.

"That's a possibility," Frank confirms.

"I agree...," Catherine states dispassionately, "...though as Logan pointed out, the perp could start to veer off their original course and deviate the age or circumstances of their target."

"How do you propose to follow up on what you've already got?" Frank asks curiously.

"Lucky for us, the Langley Royal is high tech – not only do they input all their medical records to computer files, they also have electronic rostering," Catherine informs them.

"Brilliant!" Emma smiles, distracted by the possibilities that Catherine's news opens up. "That means we can see who was on duty when the murders happened."

"Is it really that easy?" Frank asks, his brows furrowed with concern.

"It is if you know what you're doing," Catherine lifts a brow at the Inspector's doubting tone. "And I'm the best at what I do – I don't take chances and I don't leave electronic footprints. Neither of us do," she smiles over at Emma.

"I admire you girls, I really do," Frank tells them.

"But...?" Logan asks.

"But I'm a law enforcement officer – while I know that what you do is for the greater good, it is against the law," he sighs heavily.

"So...what does that mean?" Catherine asks testily.

"It means that – while I understand what you do and why you do it – I would rather not be privy to the ins and outs of your methods," he tells them guiltily.

"It comes down to 'plausible deniability'," he states. "If I'm ever asked to give evidence against you...," and he holds up a staying hand when Catherine would have jumped in, "...in the very unlikely event that you are ever caught, I can truthfully deny all knowledge of the inner workings of your operation."

Still frowning at the unintended slight on her mad skills, Catherine nods, "I suppose that's understandable, even logical – but you don't need to worry, we're excellent at what we do. While she doesn't have my singular expertise, I can vouch that Emma does have a lot of skills and is perfectly capable of doing this work."

"Thanks...," Emma frowns, "...I think!"

Logan smiles at his wife's innocent pronouncement of her tech skills – not a hint of self-aggrandisement, just a simple statement of fact, as she sees it.

Smiling at her confidence, Frank looks back at the boards with all the mounting evidence.

"I have no doubts about your skills – either of you," he adds, smiling at Catherine and then Emma. "Which is why I'm here – as soon as I can take this investigation to my Chief, I will."

Hesitating to voice his thoughts, Frank contemplates Catherine as she moves to look through a few papers on her desk.

"Catherine...I was wondering...," Frank waits for her to lift her head to look at him, then continues, "...I spoke to Neil Faraday yesterday and he's really keen to meet with you."

"Hmm," Catherine frowns suspiciously. "He's your psychic buddy, isn't he - what's he want with me?"

"If you remember, after you had that experience when you 'knew' that Edwards was about to break into the Richerson's residence, I suggested you meet with my psychic friend to see if he could help you to develop that sense," Frank reminds her, and watches Catherine grimace at the thought.

Logan watches Catherine with interest, she has an amazing mind and abilities beyond what most would ever dream of attaining, yet she appears reluctant to open herself up to this possibility. *Maybe the thought frightens her? No, that's not Catherine at all – she's as intrepid as they come. So why is she hesitating?*

"Sounds fascinating," Emma grins happily. "I didn't know you could do all that 'woowoo' stuff," she adds in a comic voice.

Throwing a hand out in Emma's direction, Catherine scoffs in disgust, "You see – that's just the sort of thing I hate. Before you know it everyone will be calling me 'freak' again!"

"I told you once that I don't want to hear that word in this house ever again...," Logan scowls, "...and I meant it! Just because you're special, just because you have a brilliant mind and maybe some other, as yet, untapped talents, doesn't mean that you are in any way a freak. You're gifted," Logan tells her more softly, walking to put a hand to her cheek. "And I love you."

Leaning her cheek into his palm, Catherine looks into Logan's eyes and nods.

"Ok, I'll see what he has to say, then I'll decide if I want to try to develop my so called gift," she tells him quietly.

"That's my girl," Logan smiles. "But if you decide to leave well alone, that's up to you. I just think it's better to make that choice with all the information you can get on the subject – and Frank trusts this man."

The Langley Royal is quiet now, compared to the rush of activity around evening meals, assisting patient's to shift their position in the beds and the last drug round of the day.

Nights can be a good time to study, and Helen has the computer on.

"What elearning are you doing?" Sister Holly Manfred asks.

"It's just the update for my Health & Safety module," Helen tells her. "Nights are a good time to get caught up on these things."

Taking a seat next to Helen, Holly looks at her with some concern. "Are you ok about Mr Weston – I know you took a liking to him?"

"He was lovely, wasn't he?" Helen smiles wistfully at her colleague. "But at least he isn't suffering now. He was in so much pain, but he was just too nice to complain."

Frowning, Holly tries to recall Mr Weston's details. "Did he actually tell you that he was in a lot of pain?"

Shaking her head, Helen turns to fully face Holly. "It's just what I observed. He would cringe with it even in his sleep. I told him that he should tell you nurses, but he always said that he didn't want to be a nuisance and that it wasn't really so bad. But it was, I saw it in his eyes."

"And did you report your observations to the nurse looking after Mr Weston?" Holly asks.

"A couple of times, but mostly I just sat with him and tried to distract him with conversations about his garden and the old dog he was missing so much," Helen smiles.

"Hmm, if I remember right, Mr Weston couldn't tolerate Morphine," Holly frowns, dredging up the information from the recesses of her mind. "In fact, he didn't react well to Opiates in general – that made his pain control tricky." Then Holly smiles pleasantly at Helen, "At least he had you to comfort and distract him – you're very good with the patients. Have you ever thought of training up to become a nurse?"

Helen is taken aback, but delighted by her senior's praise. "I...didn't think that would be possible," she admits. "I missed a lot of schooling – my father needed a lot of looking after," she reveals sadly.

"Wasn't your mother able to help you?" Holly asks with genuine concern.

"No; I'm afraid she wasn't in good health herself, so..."

I'm sorry, Helen, I didn't realise," Holly places a hand over Helen's on the desk. "Is that why you tend to gravitate towards the elderly patients?"

Realising that the Sister has obviously noticed her activities, Helen decides to try and throw her off.

"Not really, I spent quite a bit of time with Tim Givens yesterday," she smiles. "He's so funny, and very brave considering the operations he still has ahead of him."

"He really is," Holly agrees. "Tim's parents are great too; they give him a lot of support. It can't be easy having a son in his early twenties who loves motorbikes – this is his second big road accident, but by far the worst!"

"He was telling me that the surgeons are still not sure if he'll ever walk again," Helen murmurs thoughtfully.

"He certainly has got a very steep mountain to climb," Holly nods with pursed lips. "It won't be easy for a young, active man like Tim to accept life in a wheelchair, if it happens."

No, he'll wither away slowly until he disappears into a well of depression. What a terrible thought – it shouldn't be allowed to happen!

CHAPTER SIX

"Hmm, this electronic rostering is a nightmare," Catherine grumbles to no one in particular.

"Going through these medical records is no picnic either," Emma replies in the same distracted tone.

"What you girls need is a break," a female voice orders from the quietly opened door.

"Caroline, Adrianne, what are you doing here?" Catherine frowns over her laptop at them.

"We love you too," Caroline chuckles as she and Adrianne both take a seat.

"Anyone would think you're too busy for your own sisters," Adrianne chimes in. "Oh, wait, you are too busy for your own sisters...that's why we're here!"

With her frown deepening, Catherine gets up to make some coffee.

"You want some...?" she asks, holding up her mug to Emma and her sisters.

"Do you have any Lady Grey?" Caroline asks with a lifted brow.

"Of course..." Catherine tells her loftily, "...I know you rarely drink anything else these days."

"Just black decaf coffee will do me," Adrianne smiles.

"And me," Emma pipes up.

With her frown turning into a scowl, Catherine gathers mugs and turns to prepare the hot drinks.

"Don't know why you drink coffee if it doesn't have caffeine – what's the point?"

"Catherine, I hope whatever crawled up your arse and soured your mood is not going to be a permanent fixture for today. We're taking you both out for lunch and you'll shrivel the salad with a face like that," Caroline tells her sharply as she accepts her tea.

Letting out a giggle, Adrianne earns a glare as Catherine hands her a mug of coffee.

Taking Emma's drink over to her desk, Catherine continues to scowl and says, "What...you got nothing to add?"

On a low chuckle, Emma just shakes her head and sips her coffee. She may not be intimidated by Catherine, as many people are, but she knows when to keep her head down.

"So...what is the problem?" Caroline persists. "You usually love all this tech work," she adds, waving a hand in the general direction of the information pinned to the boards.

"Tech work, as you call it, is easy," Catherine proclaims confidently. "But interpreting and cross checking the information we find, that's the difficult bit."

"But you've always loved puzzles," Caroline exclaims, then looks at Catherine and frowns. "I have no idea where that came from – I just suddenly saw a picture of us playing on the floor holding large puzzle pieces in our hands."

With her jaw dropped and her eyes wide, Catherine says, "I saw it too, and mum was sat on the floor helping us."

"Gees, that's creepy," Emma grimaces dramatically. "I'm glad I don't have a twin that can see inside my head!"

But Adrianne looks forlorn. "I wish I could share your thoughts – I'd love to remember mum."

Distracted, the twins turn in unison to look at their younger sister.

"Well I do," Adrianne insists. "At least you two have your 'twin thing' – I don't have any memories of you or mum or dad. I'm an outsider," she murmurs sadly.

"Now see what you've done!" Caroline turns on

Catherine. "We were both happy as Larry till we got here – now get your jackets, or whatever else you need, and get your arses into gear. We are all going out for lunch!"

Feeling guilty for the sadness she can still see on Adrianne's pretty face, Catherine does as she's told without so much as a grumble.

"Sorry, I didn't mean to let my bad mood vent," she tells Adrianne awkwardly. "And you're not an outsider – how can you even think that."

"I don't, not really...well, not all the time anyway," she shrugs.

"Adrianne, we are family and there are no outsiders," Catherine states firmly as she gets in the front seat of Logan's car.

As spacious as his Range Rover is, Emma takes the middle back seat and feels like she's surrounded on all sides.

Smiling nervously as she watches Logan climb in behind the wheel, Emma looks at him via the rear view mirror.

"You must be feeling brave," Emma comments, and Logan turns to look at her.

"How so?"

"You have three very pregnant women in the car who could all pop at any moment," she reminds him with a nervous smile.

Looking taken aback, Logan swallows audibly. "That was not nice," he tells Emma, grimacing at her through the rear view mirror.

"Just saying..."

The drive into town doesn't take long. Even though it is almost 1 o'clock, the lunch time rush seems to be thinning out.

"So, where have you decided we're going?" Catherine asks her sisters dryly.

"The Coffee Pot – they had some delicious looking homemade cheese and ham quiche the last time I looked," Caroline says, and feels her stomach rumble at the mention of food.

Mmm, that sounds pretty good actually. Holy hell, they'd better not be dragging me off to do girl shopping – I hate shopping of any kind!

"This sudden need to take us out to lunch...," Catherine begins warily, "...wouldn't be a ruse to get me to do some kind of shopping would it?" And she turns to frown at Logan accusingly.

"Hey, this has nothing to do with me," he grins at her, amused by her unusual aversion to spending money.

"It was just lunch...but now you mention it..." Caroline muses.

"Oh, oh, we could nip into Mothercare and pick out

your nursery," Adrianne suggests excitedly. "You said you wanted to get started on that room next," she reminds Caroline, who is in charge of all the redecorating of the new suite of rooms that Catherine, Logan and Mrs Baines are to move into at Lakelands.

"That's a great idea," Caroline leans forward to smile across Emma to her sister.

"Should'a kept my mouth shut," Catherine grumbles quietly, making Logan chuckle.

"Don't know what you're laughing at, you're coming with us," Catherine smirks with satisfaction, then frowns when she sees Logan shake his head.

"Sorry, nothing I would like more...," Logan lies easily, "...but I'm going to drop you girls off then take the opportunity to go into the office for a couple of hours."

Moments later Catherine is standing on the pavement glaring at the rear end of the Range Rover as Logan makes his escape.

I'll remember this...traitor!

"Hey, look...," Adrianne points to something in the café's window, "...we have got to leave room for some of that!"

Turning with her frown still in place, Catherine looks in the direction Adrianne is pointing, and drools longingly.

"Too right!" she agrees, her taste-buds going into

overdrive at the sight of a gooey chocolate gateau with all the trimmings.

Only Emma looks reticent at the idea. "Some of us still have a waistline to think about."

Taking the lead, Catherine smiles broadly, "Then you can just watch us eat it and weep."

Adrianne and Caroline both giggle at Emma's predicament but are looking forward to desert.

"Did you look at those fabric samples I left you?" Caroline asks Catherine just as she spoons in another mouthful of gateau.

Swallowing quickly, Catherine nods obediently. "Why do you do that – it's like you wait until I put food in my mouth then ask a question you know I can't answer!"

Laughing, Caroline is unrepentant. "The fabric, Catherine, did you pick out any favourites?"

"Let's put it this way – I took out the ones I really didn't like, the rest is up to you," Catherine states firmly.

Emma shakes her head in disbelief. "You have the chance to refurb' an entire wing of a very large house with your own choice of furnishings and yet you're leaving it to your sister... I'd be running from shop to shop with a manic grin on my face," she laughs as Catherine grimaces.

"Well, feel free to help Caroline," Catherine tells her. "As a matter of fact, don't you have some refurbishing of your own to do?"

Looking quizzical and at a loss, Emma just stares and shakes her head.

"The gatehouse – it's nearly finished being renovated, now all you have to do is tart it up," Catherine tells her with some satisfaction.

"You mean...I get to choose new furniture, carpets and curtains and stuff," Emma gapes open mouthed.

"Hah, and you thought I was the only one lumbered with shopping," Catherine smirks.

But Emma is far from displeased. Looking at Caroline, she beams from ear to ear.

"When do we start – this is great!"

"What..." Catherine is dumbstruck, then purses her lips in a stubborn pout. "Am I the only sane female around here? Gees, you girlies go knock yourselves out, I'm going to get a taxi back and get some work done!"

"You really don't mind...?" Emma asks uncertainly, after all this is meant to be a work day and they are working on her aunt's case.

"Go for it...," Catherine tells her, then grins mischievously, "...I'll let you pick up my lunch bill to make up for it.

"That is a deal," Emma grins happily.

The house is cold when Helen gets home from work. But that is nothing new, her mother has never liked the central heating on so Helen is used to living in the near freezing conditions.

Picking the post up off the floor she looks through it distractedly.

"I'm home," she calls up the stairs then removes her coat and hangs it in the hall closet. "I'll make you a cup of tea and bring it up."

Moving to the kitchen she methodically makes the tea, wiping the meticulously clean work-surfaces of any residue.

With care not to spill any in the saucer, Helen carries the tea up the stairs to the main bedroom.

"Here you go," she smiles, placing the cup and saucer on the bedside table. "I had a good day at work today," she tells her beloved mother. "One of the Sister's thinks I'd make a good nurse; she asked if I'd ever thought of qualifying," she says proudly as she goes about tidying the room and straightening the bedding.

"I'll get your bowl and a towel, then I'll freshen you up, ok?" she smiles tenderly and strokes her mother's hair back from her forehead.

Going to the bathroom, Helen starts to sing a tune her mother used to sing around the house. It comforts her, bringing back memories of happier times when her mother hadn't been bedridden.

Now she has her work, and under the guidance of her precious mother, Helen carries it out in the name of the Lord and for the sake of mercy.

"Ok, I've tested the water and it's cool, just the way you like it," she states as she pulls up a small table and sets the bowl down on it, seating herself on the side of her mother's bed.

Gently, Helen takes a soft cloth and bathes her mother's face. "There, that's better isn't it? You didn't drink all the milk I left you this morning; you'll never get better if you don't at least drink your milk," she chides softly. "You've been so good to me, teaching me and guiding me when I didn't know which way to turn - I couldn't bear it if anything happened to you, so you be good now."

Continuing to recount her day and details about the patients she has been looking after, Helen goes about the task of freshening her mother up.

"You'd like Hetty Longeaton, she's in her sixties and is so funny," Helen chuckles. "She has dementia and keeps telling her 6'2" sons off like they are 6 year olds, but she has a good heart," Helen smiles, thinking kindly of the woman. "I swear, she can remember what she did 50 years ago better than she can remember what she did in the last 5 minutes. But she seems happy enough and her sons clearly love her."

Helen looks lovingly down at the woman in the bed and gently brushes back her hair.

Then her eyes cloud over as she remembers another patient, one who has all his faculties and will suffer all the more for that fact when he's stuck in a wheelchair for the rest of his life.

"There's another patient, a young man in his early twenties, he had a really bad road accident. He was riding a motorbike," Helen shakes her head, wondering why boys always want to do the dangerous things and put their lives needlessly at risk.

"Well, it doesn't sound like he'll ever ride it again," she speculates sadly. "He will almost certainly never walk again...ever..."

"Do you think he needs your help?" her mother asks.

"I don't know...I only usually help those people who have no one else to help them. The ones suffering as you do."

If only the doctors would do their job – it's wrong to leave people suffering in such pain. An owner would be prosecuted for leaving a dog to suffer that way, why are people not allowed the same dignity and help?

"It is your calling - you can't ignore what God asks of you."

"Yes, I know, it's just that he's so young."

"It isn't your place to decide who needs your help! It is God's work you do, now listen to him when he guides you and act accordingly."

"You're right, I see that now. I'll do as you say, I'll help him as soon as I'm able," Helen assures her mother obediently.

Bye the time Emma gets back to the office, Catherine has found another probable victim and it's troubling her.

But Emma is buzzing from her shopping spree with Catherine's sisters.

"I don't believe what I just bought on your accounts," Emma goggles, her mind recalling the two sumptuous settees and the bed along with all the bedding she would ever need and draperies to match. "Caroline assured me you wouldn't mind, but...what's wrong?" she asks, finally realising that Catherine is upset at something.

Pointing to the board, Catherine tells her about the latest patient she's found to have died in suspicious circumstances.

"She was 71, has a bunch of children and grandchildren – there's probably even a couple of great-grandchildren," Catherine tells Emma sadly. "This isn't just about the victims; it's about the families that have had to suffer the loss when it wasn't necessary - not until someone decided to end them, damn it!"

Walking to the board, Emma reads the notes for herself and has to agree. "There was nothing; no diabetes or heart-failure, not even high blood-pressure." Turning to face Catherine, Emma looks determined, "I think it's time to do more than just search for victims."

With a frown, Catherine tilts her head to one side and asks, "What do you suggest, a leaked story to the press – I don't think Frank would appreciate that."

"This is not about what Frank wants anymore," Emma insists. "It's about getting an official investigation started – we can't do this on our own!"

Biting on her bottom lip, Catherine paces then nods in agreement. "We can pretend to be a worried relative – say we want to remain anonymous because of the possible backlash. I doubt the press would need much more than that to publish a vague accusation under the guise of concern."

Hauling in a breath, Emma let's it out slowly, the enormity of what they are planning to do hitting home.

"I'll do it," she offers. "I can do a good northern'ish accent so I won't be recognised."

Catherine looks at her warily, "So, you're telling me you're a good liar, is that it?"

Lifting her chin, Emma firms her lips and puts her hands on her hips. "If the need calls for it, I can bluff my way out of a sticky situation. But I'm sure it can't be that difficult to play a role on the other end of a telephone – it's not like they'll be able to see me blushing," Emma frowns in annoyance.

"Hey, you offered," Catherine reminds her. "So where are you planning to phone from?"

"What?" Emma turns her frown on her desk and the telephone sat on it. "Oh. I suppose I'll have to go to a payphone," she muses.

"Not too local," Catherine warns.

Looking at her blankly, Emma twigs what she means and rolls her eyes. "You mean you want me to drive to the next village or something?"

"Makes sense...you don't want it tracing back here...to us," Catherine rationalises.

"Ok...I'll go now and get it done," Emma nods, her stance now determined. Picking up her car keys and mobile, she walks to the door then turns back to look at Catherine. "We're going to stop this monster, Catherine...we just need to reach out for some help from the experts."

CHAPTER SEVEN

With her head bent over her laptop, Catherine doesn't see Logan at the door of the office watching her.

She has printed off all of the rosters of the nursing and medical staff at the times when patients are thought to have been murdered.

"Hi," Logan says softly so as not to make her jump. And when she lifts her head to look at him he smiles, though his eyes are filled with concern.

Crossing the room, Logan moves around her desk to kiss Catherine before taking a seat.

"Sorry, I know I'm not being very sociable...," Catherine frowns across the desk to her very understanding husband, "...but I need to work this a little while longer."

"What are you trying to do?" he asks, genuinely interested.

"I'm trying to narrow down a list of staff that would have had the opportunity to kill their patients," she explains. "But you would not believe the number of staff that work on these wards, or the different shift patterns that have to be accommodated."

Getting to her feet, she crosses to one of the large whiteboards and writes a list of the shift patterns worked on the Orthopaedics ward.

"You've got the early shift, from 07.15 to 14.45, then the late shift which starts at 12.45 to 20.15. The shifts have an overlap to allow for teaching sessions and for them to relieve each other for lunch breaks," she explains.

"But as well as those two shifts you have people who do long days," she tells him. "They work straight through from 07.15 to 20.15, a 13 hour shift with 2 half hour breaks."

"That's a very long day," Logan comments, his brows drawing together.

"Hmm, not for the faint hearted, I'm sure," Catherine agrees, then moves to fill in the last shift pattern. "Nights are just as long – they start at 19.45 and finish at 07.45 with the same amount of breaks as the long day people."

"And you've been able to cross reference the patients date and time of death to the staff on duty?" Logan asks.

"That's what I'm in the middle of doing," Catherine

nods. "Trouble is, as well as doing their contracted hours, a lot of them are also 'Bank Staff' – which means they work extra shifts when the hospital needs them, and not always on their own ward."

She adds this information to the board.

"Christ," Logan groans, "then you could have victims on other wards!"

"Exactly," Catherine agrees, taking a step back from the board to look at her list.

"It's a good job this investigation has been made official," Logan observes, his head slowly shaking from side to side. Then he lifts a hand, palm outwards, when Catherine spins to stare at him, annoyance written plainly on her lovely face.

"I just meant that this is going to get extremely complicated," he tells her placatingly. "I'm not questioning yours or Emma's abilities, but many hands make light work – and it will let you concentrate on the Orthopaedics ward. At least, that's what I'd do," he adds when Catherine continues to frown.

Then she completely surprises him by agreeing. "You're right, of course. We'll have enough to do with what we've already got – but I'm glad Frank has been assigned the case."

"Wow, did you just say 'you're right'," Logan chuckles softly

"Funny guy," she rolls her eyes then joins in with his laughter. "Don't let it go to your head, clever-clogs!"

When he takes her in his arms, Logan's laughter stills, "I'm so proud of you. After everything, all you ever want to do is help people."

"Why not, it's how I earn a living," Catherine shrugs.

"You can be as blasé as you like with others, but not with me, Catherine." Logan looks into her lovely blue eyes until she gives him a silent nod. "Good, because I love the woman you are. Even though you're often bullish, sometimes petulant and hellishly caustic when your temper's riled...," he smiles as Catherine purses her lips and lifts a brow, "...but the flip side of that makes it all worthwhile. You protect those you love and I sometimes can't believe my luck that I'm among them."

Her annoyance at his description of her, though admittedly accurate, dissipates in a moment as she reaches up to touch his beautiful face.

"I'd ask you if you're crazy, but that's a given seeing as how you were fool enough to take up with me," she smiles adoringly. "I know I'm not the easiest person to be around; when I get scared I get angry, and loving you is the scariest thing I've ever done."

Standing on tiptoe, Catherine puts her lips gently to his and moves her hand round to the back of his head to hold him to her.

Pouring her heart into the kiss, Catherine attempts to show him how she feels rather than using useless words that can only fall short.

When they draw apart Logan feels like he's been pole-axed. "Loving you is the best thing I've ever done, or ever will do."

Taking a step back, Catherine smiles up at him mischievously, "In that case, you won't mind coming with me when I go to meet Frank and his psychic buddy!"

"That's today..?"

"Don't you tell me that you can't make it," she warns darkly. "I refuse to talk woowoo with a complete stranger on my own!"

"Woowoo?" Logan laughs at her turn of phrase.

"Well that's what Emma called it, if you remember," she recalls, not liking the way it had made her feel.

"Yes, I remember now," Logan frowns, nodding his head. "Just you remember what I told you – no matter what you find out about yourself and your abilities today, I don't want to hear the 'f' word ever again. Got it?"

When she nods, he draws her to him again. "Good, then I'll happily come with you. What time do we need to leave?"

"Not for an hour yet," Catherine informs him. "Emma will be here in a minute, I'll catch her up on what I've been doing and then I'll come down. Ok?"

They are meeting Inspector Frank Harper at Neil Faraday's house. Logan is driving while Catherine sits fidgeting beside him.

"He isn't going to do anything you don't want," Logan assures her, trying to calm Catherine's evident nerves.

"So you say!"

"So Frank says," Logan insists. But before he gets to the house, he pulls the Range Rover over to the side of the road and turns to look at Catherine. "If you really don't want to go through with this, I'll take you home right now," he offers.

"But..."

"But...," he echoes on a sigh, "...I want you to think about our boys. If whatever this is passes on to them, how will you be able to help them to deal with it if you don't understand it yourself?"

Shocked by the suggestion that she might pass on her so called 'gift' to her boys, Catherine stares back at Logan open mouthed.

"You make it sound like I've got some kind of a disease that I'm infecting them with," she eventually gets out.

"Don't say that," he reprimands sharply. "And you know that isn't what I meant at all. I just want you to consider the possibility that our boys may have to deal with what you did as a child – you struggled all alone, our boys won't have to!"

"You know that's emotional blackmail," she accuses quietly, then falls silent while she mulls his suggestion over.

Pursing her lips, Catherine looks over at Logan with grim determination. "If he starts trying to get me to perform like some circus animal, I'm walking out!"

Nodding in agreement, and heaving a discreet sigh of relief, Logan turns in his seat and pulls away from the curb.

When they pull up outside of Neil Faraday's house they can see that the inspector is already there.

"That's Frank's car," Catherine points to the second car on the drive of the semi-detached house they are about to visit.

Taking hold of her hand, Logan walks Catherine down the slabbed pathway alongside the drive and up to the front door.

"You really think this is a good idea?" she asks nervously, a hand unconsciously going to the swell of her belly at the thought of her boys.

"I do," Logan assures her. "If you decide you can't learn anything from this man then at least you will have made the effort to meet him. However, from what Frank said, it's entirely possible that he can help you to control and maybe even develop your ability."

"Assuming I have any," she grumbles with a frown.

"Alright...," Logan decides not to argue the point, "...we'll just go in with open minds and see what we see – if that's nothing, then so be it."

But nothing is far from what she feels when Neil Faraday shakes her hand in welcome.

Managing to keep the jolt she felt right through her body to herself, Catherine merely smiles and says, "Hello, nice to meet you."

But Neil had felt the same jolt and isn't convinced by her bravado.

So, you don't trust me...be that as it may you felt what I did. In time you'll share your secrets with me, but for now...

"Let's take a seat and get to know one another," he suggests with a friendly smile.

"What do you want to know?" Catherine asks suspiciously, her tone wary.

Neil shrugs, "Anything you care to share with me."

Tricky! Tricky! Now I'm forced to tell you something...but what?

"Sometimes, when I was in junior school, I'd know things without realising that I knew them," she tells him, then sighs and tells him the rest. "I once told a girl that I was sorry about her mum – she'd died in a car wreck – only it hadn't happened yet."

Frowning at the uncomfortable memory, Catherine falls silent.

"That must have been awkward," Neil observes. "How long after did it actually happen?"

"When she got home her father told her that her mum had died on the way to work that morning, so…I don't know," Catherine muses. "I seemed to wake up already knowing. It didn't occur to me that no one had told me or that I hadn't read it somewhere."

"Was that the first time you experienced precognition?" he asks gently.

Catherine shakes her head. "I don't remember any specific times prior to that, but I remember my mum asking how I knew this or that, like she was surprised." Shrugging her shoulders, she turns to look at Logan and he smiles reassuringly.

"And after that incident – were there more times as specific as that had been?"

Feeling her chest tighten, Catherine has to force herself to think back over events she has tried hard to bury.

Nodding, she tells Neil, "It wasn't always bad news, or

even important." Then a smile tugs at the side of her lips and she chuckles quietly. "There was a girl at school, real athletic type and beautiful too. Everyone seemed to hang on her opinions and treated her like she was something special. This one time, she was bragging about how her netball team was going to wipe the floor with the competition in the big final that was coming up."

Turning her grin on Logan she tells him, "I couldn't resist it – I just laughed and told her 'In your dreams, Daphne', and she just stared after me with her haughty nose in the air."

Joining in with her chuckle, Logan asks, "And did they lose?"

"And then some! Daphne was team captain and had her worst game ever," Catherine remembers, her grin widening.

And she deserved the stick she took over it for the next few weeks. Daphne Manson was one of the cruellest people it was my misfortune to know during school.

"And since then, as an adult, have you had any more specific episodes?" Neil asks.

Shaking her head, Catherine shrugs.

Then Frank coughs, getting her attention and lifts his brow. "What about Edwards?" he reminds her gently.

When Catherine drops her eyes to contemplate the

pattern on his carpet, Neil decides it's time he gave something of himself.

"I didn't have your experiences as a child," Neil begins, and notices Catherine's slight head movement to show that she is listening. "My abilities were a bit of a shock, actually. I went in for surgery and 'died' on the operating table."

At that, Catherine looks up and over at Neil, a question in her eyes.

"It took so long to get me back that the doctors were all sure that I would have suffered brain damage through lack of oxygen," he grimaces at the thought. "And maybe they were right, just not in the way they expected."

"And...that's when it started for you?" Catherine asks quietly, watching Neil nod. "That must have been scary. But when did you first know that you were 'different' – did something happen in the hospital?"

"No. Thankfully," Neil's smile is just short of a grimace. "I think the drugs they had me on were too strong to let my mind do any serious thinking. But when I got home..."

The grimace is fully in place as Neil remembers his first 'insight'.

The room remains silent, it's occupants sensing that Neil needs the time to pull his thoughts together.

"It was worse than any film you've ever watched – in

them the person gets a flash of a tragic scene before it's happened and calls the police to warn them," Neil shakes his head and lets out a dull mocking chuckle.

"I had just gotten into the shower...," he begins again, "...one minute I was enjoying the heat of the water and the feeling of being back in familiar surroundings, the next I was walking among the dead and listening to the survivors of a train wreck's screams."

"Walking among...?" Catherine asks.

"Yes, quite literally, I assure you," Neil nods and makes deliberate eye contact with Catherine. "That's why it was so horrific, so traumatic to come to terms with when it was over. I don't just see the vision; I become a part of it."

Letting out a long sigh, Catherine frowns then smiles over at Neil.

"Hell, I'm just a lightweight compared to you," she chuckles softly. "Mine is more feelings and flashes, I've never walked inside a vision and I don't think I ever want to."

Smiling now, glad that Catherine appears more relaxed and comfortable after hearing his story, Neil asks her to sit with him at the dining table. "I just want to try something very basic," he assures her when a wary shadow falls again.

Sensing that this should be just the two of them, Frank and Logan remain seated in the lounge area of the long room and watch closely as the two take their seats at the dining table.

"You're not going to start any woowoo stuff, are you?" Catherine asks before Neil can begin. "Cuz if you are, I'm off!" and she casts Logan a worried glance.

"No woowoo, I promise," Neil smiles reassuringly. "All I want to do is try to repeat the connection we had when you first arrived and we shook hands."

Her eyes snap back to his and her cheeks begin to pink. *Damn it, I didn't think you'd noticed that! You hid it better than I did, apparently.*

"How?" she asks simply, not bothering to deny it.

"I just want to take both your hands and see what we see – or not," he tells her.

Reaching both her hands across the table, Catherine waits for him to take them in his and holds her breath, waiting to be zapped by lightening, or something.

But there was nothing...nothing at all.

CHAPTER EIGHT

"Well that was a big fat waste of time," Catherine flounces down on a settee in their lounge and looks up at Logan with annoyance marring her beautiful face.

"I wouldn't say that," he contradicts. "You did have a connection with Neil; it just didn't happen when you tried to do it deliberately."

"So you think he's right, we connected because I wasn't expecting it, wasn't already tensed up and blocking him?"

"I think that sounds reasonable."

"So you think I should go back...," Catherine states rather than asks.

"I do," Logan tells her frankly. "But it's what you think that counts."

Well that's a load of bull! You want me to go back and

learn all I can about this 'ability', if only for the sake of the boys.

I'm not so sure. What if I start working with Neil and I end up walking in visions the way he does – I don't think I could cope with that!

I wouldn't want to cope with that!

"You do realise that working with Neil could make things worse," Catherine raises a brow as she turns to her husband. "Do you really want to unleash something that neither of us understands?"

Taking her hand, Logan lifts it to his lips then continues to hold it. "That could happen with or without Neil – he told you that, he's seen it happen before."

"So he says!" Catherine shifts uncomfortably.

"I had a good feeling about Neil," Logan gives her hand a gentle squeeze. "And, if I'm not mistaken, you did too."

What, is everyone psychic now!

But she knows that he is right. Neil had been sincere in his beliefs and somewhere deep inside, she trusted him.

"Ok, ok, so I'll go back. But that doesn't mean it will work!"

"Just give it time," Logan leans forward to kiss her pouting lips. "I think Neil is right, the connection will come when you are able to relax with him."

Heaving a long sigh, Catherine gets to her feet and looks up at Logan as he comes to stand beside her.

"I need to get my head back into normal," she states abruptly. "For me that's my computer and whatever I can find on it."

Moving a large, gentle hand to cup her cheek, Logan dips his head to take her lips again.

"I love you, Catherine. You and all your little foibles make my life wonderful," he tells her, his thumb gently caressing her cheek.

"Gees, I actually believe you mean that," she smiles in amazement.

"You'd better believe it. There is nothing about you that will frighten me away or disgust me, or whatever else your brilliant mind is telling you will happen if you learn to use this ability you have," he tells her more firmly. "We are together forever – and we'll learn to deal with this together also. So no more worrying!"

You say that now, but you might come to see me as a freak, just like 'they' did back in school. You can't un-see what you've already seen, so there would be no going back once we start this.

"Ok, no more worrying," she agrees.

When Emma looks up as Catherine enters their office, she is struck by her expression.

"What's wrong, did the woowoo man upset you?" Emma asks, feeling protective of Catherine.

"What...? No...," Catherine replies as she walks over to make a mug of coffee. Looking back at Emma she holds her mug up and asks, "You want one?"

"Yes, coffee, black," Emma replies, watching her friend and colleague perform the task in total silence.

Having passed the mug of coffee over to Emma, Catherine takes her own and sits behind her desk and doesn't even open her laptop.

"Ok, give," Emma demands coming to stand in front of Catherine. "You never sit there without your laptop open, it just doesn't happen. So what did he do to spook you?!"

"He didn't 'do' anything," Catherine affirms. "I'm just not sure about all this stuff."

"Not sure...as in, whether or not you want to meet up with him again?"

Nodding, Catherine frowns up at Emma and says, "If we're going to talk about this at least take a seat – you're giving me a crick in my neck," she snaps grumpily.

Having gotten to know Catherine quite well in the last few weeks, Emma knows that she tends to get angry when she's upset or frightened, so doesn't take her tone personally.

Dragging over a chair, Emma sits then looks at Catherine expectantly.

"Nothing happened, not really, but he told me about his own experiences...Jesus, they scared me to death," Catherine admits in a rush.

"Why, what was so bad about them – does he see dead people?" Emma asks with a shiver and a grimace.

"In a way, yes," Catherine surprises her. "He doesn't just have visions of something that's going to happen – he actually walks in the midst of it, can hear and smell everything around him. He just can't touch or make himself known to anyone. He's the one who is like a ghost walking amongst the carnage."

"Sounds very spooky...," Emma admits, "...and you're worried that you could end up doing the same?"

"Hmm, or something similar," Catherine admits. "I don't want any of this, Emma - why can't I just carry on ignoring it as I have been doing for the last few years, damn it!"

"I don't know...," Emma tells her and shrugs, not having any idea why she can't do just that.

"Because Logan thinks I need to understand it in case the boys are born with the same ability," Catherine tells her angrily.

"And you disagree...?"

"No...not exactly," Catherine frowns into her coffee, her thoughts as clear as mud. "But that doesn't mean I want to develop it either!"

"Well, you said nothing happened...maybe nothing will happen," Emma says optimistically.

Catherine grimaces as she looks over at Emma. "I lied," she admits shame faced. "When we first shook hands I felt something jolt through me – and no, it wasn't attraction," she dismisses firmly.

"Well you did tell me that it was what happened when you first met Logan," Emma defends easily. "And I know it's what I felt when I first met Sloane."

"I could never feel that way about anyone other than Logan," Catherine shakes her head firmly. "He's why I take my next breath – he's essential to my being, to my survival!"

"Wow, that's heavy."

"No, it really isn't, it's just the way it is between us," Catherine smiles.

"Then you're a very lucky woman."

"Yes...I know it."

"So what do you intend to do about the woowoo guy?" Emma chuckles as Catherine grimaces comically.

"Will you stop calling him that...it gives me the creeps," Catherine frowns. "And I don't know what I'm going to do – I'll have to give it some thought. Maybe I'll ask my sisters what they think about all this. Either of them has more life experience than I have!"

"Ok, so back to the matter in hand," Emma decides to distract Catherine from her troubled thoughts. "I've used your printouts of the duty rosters to narrow down the staff who were on duty at the time of each of the deaths we've added to our board," she begins, all business now.

"Unbelievably there are only 11 out of all of the staff over that time period who were on duty at an opportune time."

"11, that's more than I thought," Catherine looks at the list Emma gives her.

"And that is only accounting for staff that have direct patient access," Emma clarifies. "There are no porters or domestics on that list."

"Ok, that sounds reasonable. We'll only widen the investigation out if we come up short with these," Catherine nods as she reads the names on the list.

"The ratio of females to males is about what you'd expect considering that it's still a female dominated occupation on the nursing side," Emma explains. "The medics are another deal altogether – doctors are mostly male, although the female ratio is improving."

"What are these?" Catherine leans over her desk, pointing to the list under the initials, HCA's.

"Health Care Assistants," Emma explains. "They are care givers, they do observations and sometimes help with relatives, offering comfort and making the obligatory cup of tea."

"So, they're hands on?" Catherine frowns.

"Very much so, according to their experience," Emma nods. "They do a lot of the personal care, like assisting with washes."

"That's certainly up close and personal and gives them ample opportunity," Catherine observes.

"There are only 2 of them who have been there long enough to have carried out the murders-"

"Suspected murders," Catherine corrects.

"Ok, ok. Suspected murders," Emma frowns back at Catherine. "The nursing staff accounts for most of the other contenders as the medics rotate. The 3 you've got listed there are Consultants with 1 Special Registrar."

"Have you started on doing background checks?" Catherine asks, studying the list as if one name might jump out at her.

Psychic...huh...I'm not getting any hints from this list and I'm bloody concentrating!

"Not yet, no," Emma sighs.

"Have you heard anything from Frank or Shivers?" Catherine asks, still concentrating on the list of names.

But before Emma can answer the telephones start to ring.

The girls frown over at each other as they answer them, one speaking to Shivers, the other to Frank Harper.

"Yes," Catherine tells Frank when he asks if they can come over for an update on their progress. "But...do you have to bring your sidekick?"

Listening to Frank's laughter, Catherine watches Emma frown at her comment.

"I would like Shivers to accompany me...," Frank tells her, "...if you can see your way clear to indulging me?"

Bloody Nora! "Alright, alright! Gees!"

"Would now be too soon?" Frank enquires hopefully.

"No, come on over," she agrees on a sigh.

A moment later Emma puts her phone down and turns to Catherine with her bottom jaw dropped in awe.

"That was more than uncanny," she declares, her eyes wide.

"You think...?" Catherine grimaces uncertainly.

Nodding enthusiastically, Emma says, "You're so used to ignoring your gift you don't recognise when it's working for you!"

"But I've been studying this list for a clue and I didn't get a whiff of anything," Catherine states, her voice filled with frustration.

"Well...I have no idea how these things work, but...maybe it worked because you weren't trying," Emma suggests hopefully.

Catherine is still frowning, looking down at the list of names she tries to clear her mind and takes a few calming breaths to steady herself.

After a full minute of staring at the list, Catherine lets out a huff of annoyance.

"This is stupid! I feel like a flaming idiot!"

Emma chuckles softly and doesn't stop when Catherine rounds on her.

"Stop taking yourself so seriously...," Emma advises, finally sobering, "...it really doesn't matter one way or the other. Either you get some insight from your gift or we do it the fun way and continue gathering info and analysing it!"

"I suppose," Catherine concedes none too graciously. "But it's frustrating – one minute I get a nudge that tells me Harper and Shivers are about to call, but when it comes to the important stuff...nothing...nada...zilch!"

Both girls' heads lift and turn to the door when they hear the front door bell sound.

Moments later a tap on the door precedes Frank Harper and Sloane Shivers' entrance to their office.

"Catherine...," Frank Harper crosses the room to take her hand, "...good to see you. And I'm very happy to say that the investigation is now very much underway and we have already begun to ask the awkward questions."

"Sounds good," Catherine tells him, and flicks a glance over at Shivers giving him a silent nod of acknowledgement.

Turning to Emma, who is still sat behind her desk, Catherine eyes her curiously.

What the hell...do I have to do this all by myself, or what!

But without saying a word, she crosses to her desk and picks up the list of possible suspects and hands it to Frank.

"We got the rosters for all the staff that work with the patients and were employed over the relevant time period," Catherine explains. "Emma has cross referenced them with the deaths we've identified as suspicious and narrowed it down to those 11 people."

"Impressive...," Frank reads the list with a raised brow, "...they have yet to hand the staff rosters over to us. You're a good jump ahead of us on this."

On hearing Shivers give a derogatory snort, Catherine peers round Frank to glare at him. "Are we going to have problems with you over this?"

"He's the boss," Sloane Shivers jerks a thumb in Frank's direction. "I just do as I'm told."

Moving to stand almost toe to toe with the tall lean detective, Catherine looks him straight in the eyes.

"No, not this time," she states flatly. "Either you're on board with this or you leave. Now!"

The room is heavy with expectation, the silence as loud as the toll of Big Ben.

"Let's just say I'm not making any objection," Shivers tells her, his voice low and dangerous.

But Catherine isn't in the mood to back down. "No, let's not!" she tells him just as quietly with a sliver of ice in her voice. "It's time you jumped off of that fence you sit on when it's convenient to do so – either you're in all the way or you get out," and her arm shoots out to point at the door.

His eyes narrowing, Shivers takes one step forward, bringing him to stand within an inch of Catherine's baby bump.

"I do not sit on fences," he leans down to growl the words close to her ear. "So to clarify...I'm in!"

"Good to know," Catherine dismisses, turning her back on him and walking over to talk to Frank like they'd never been interrupted.

Sloane's silver grey eyes sparkle with anger, but he swallows it down for the sake of getting the job done.

Emma watches as he walks stiff and tall towards her, her eyes openly devouring him.

"I don't know how you work with that woman," he growls softly.

Lifting an eyebrow, she shakes her head slowly. "You just rub her up the wrong way."

"I'm a cop, this whole set up rubs me up the wrong way," he tells her, his eyes darkening. "I just wish you weren't a part of it."

Lifting her chin, Emma comes from behind her desk to stand next to him. "Well I am, and that isn't going to change. Catherine made me a partner, so you just have to deal!"

As she walks across the room to Catherine and Frank, Emma hears his low oath.

"Shit!"

CHAPTER NINE

"So, what did your pathologist friend say when you told him the investigation was officially underway?" Catherine asks Frank.

"He admitted that he was glad it wasn't him that had started the ball rolling, but he was very happy to hear that it had gotten underway," Frank tells her. "He also said he'd go back through the cases that he'd previously thought suspect and pass the details on to me."

"He remembers them all?" Catherine asks somewhat sceptical.

"I doubt it. But if I know Carl, he'll have kept some kind of record of his concerns," Frank smiles and nods. "He may even have kept some of the biological samples and toxicology specimens – though that's probably hoping for a lot," he admits.

"It doesn't hurt to hope," Catherine smiles, and suddenly feels full of it.

Her smile is so bright and unexpected that even Sloane Shivers is dazzled by it.

Jesus...she's beautiful! I've never thought that about her before!

At that precise moment, Logan steps into the office and catches the look. It turns his heart over to see Catherine smiling so brightly that her blue eyes sparkle with it.

"You look happy," he tells her, putting a proprietorial hand to the small of Catherine's back and standing close beside her.

Turning her brightest smile up to her extremely handsome husband, Catherine moves her arm to encircle his waist.

"I think it's just the relief of having these guys on board," she tells him with a flick of her hand in the general direction of Frank and Sloane Shivers. "There's a lot we can do to help, but they're the experts."

Sloane's brow creases as he regards Catherine. He's never heard her voice this kind of opinion before.

"You really mean that?" he asks, watching her for signs of duplicity.

Her megawatt smile dims as she turns to look at the

detective, "Of course I mean that! I might have a brilliant mind but I know my limitations!"

Everyone pulls in the chuckles that want to escape at Catherine's self proclaimed brilliance, but they know she is only stating a fact. She has a massive IQ; her brain is like blotting paper for all kinds of information. She can recall facts and figures from texts she read years ago.

But Catherine is not a people person, she doesn't understand them and isn't comfortable with emotional displays that require her to respond. And tact...is a useless waste of time as far as Catherine is concerned. Her philosophy is 'say what you mean and mean what you say', for her it's just that simple.

Then she causes all eyes to drop to her protruding stomach as she lets out a groan and puts a hand to it.

"What?!" Logan looks down anxiously at his wife, his lovely brown eyes now wide and round.

"It's nothing...I probably just need to sit down for a bit," she dismisses, but everyone is still holding their breath when Sloane quickly brings a chair to the back of her.

But when she looks up and takes in all the worried faces staring at her expectantly, she has to chuckle, "Well you try carting two babies around in your belly for 9 months...then see if you don't need to take the weight off your feet now and then!"

The small group lets out a collective breath as they realise that Catherine hasn't gone into labour.

"I'm sure you're quite right, my dear," Frank Harper smiles kindly. "Are you comfortable enough to continue or would you like us to come back after you've rested a while?"

As considerate as Frank is, Catherine knows the urgency of the investigation she has been instrumental in starting.

"I'm fine, Frank. Now...you were telling us about your Pathologist friend," she recalls, focusing everyone's attention back on the case. "If he's as good at his job as you seem to think, I'll bet he's kept all of the samples he took on the cases he was concerned about."

Nodding, considering the board and all the cases they have got displayed on it, Frank agrees.

"Yes, yes I think you might be right. He's a very methodically minded chap, quite brilliant at his job."

"Ok, at least we have that on our side," Catherine sighs. "But the rest; I'll bet you haven't found getting interviews with the staff at the hospital easy to come by. They're going to close ranks and cover each other's backs!"

"That will only happen until we make them realise that catching the perpetrator is in their interests," Sloane states, but nods to acknowledge that she's right. "Once they know that we're not on a witch hunt, they'll open up – after all, they don't want the finger of suspicion hanging over them any longer than it needs to be."

"You're right – I hadn't considered that," Catherine muses as she looks up at Sloane. "You could be really useful if you weren't such a stiff shirt. Still...we'll see."

Unable to hide her smile, Emma moves to Sloane's side. "Just take it as a compliment – from Catherine it really was."

"I'd like a copy of this list you've drawn up," Frank tells Catherine and Emma. "As I said, we haven't been able to get our hands on a copy of the staff rosters as yet."

"Take that one," Emma tells him. "We have more copies and it's on the computers."

Nodding her agreement, Catherine explains, "We haven't had time to start any background checks – that took a lot of work to draw up."

"Catherine could probably have done it in half the time...," Emma concedes modestly, "...but she had a lot on so I had a go and went over my findings a dozen times to make sure I'd got it right."

"You're thorough; nothing wrong with that!" Catherine frowns up at Sloane, daring him to contradict her.

When he doesn't she turns to Logan, "Are you here to help or are you just checking up on me?"

Giving her an indulgent smile, Logan dips his head in a small bow. "Your wish is my command."

"Yeah right," she lifts a sceptical brow at him. "Well, if you've got nothing better to do you can start reading through all of the medical notes we've printed off on these people," and she points to the board bearing the names of their suspected victims.

"We didn't print off their complete records – just the last year. But if you think you need more we can get it," she tells him confidently.

"And what will I be looking for?" Logan asks.

"I have no idea," Catherine states matter of fact. "We haven't found a common denominator linking these people – just their age and the fact that they were all patients on the Orthopaedic's ward."

Turning to the two police officers, Catherine expands on her thoughts. "We're sticking to looking at these patients only – but if our perp has worked on other wards we're aware there may be more victims."

"Sensible," Sloane agrees. "We'll obviously be running our own background checks on these people, as well as drawing up our own list of suspects when we finally get the staff rosters from the hospital. If we find any likely candidates that have worked on other wards we'll follow that up."

"It might be an idea to write up a synopsis of their age, sex, living arrangements, and past medical history next to their names on your boards," Frank suggests. "It's surprising what connections can be made through visualising it all together; makes it easier to spot any possible links."

"That's a good idea," Emma nods and turns to Logan. "If you like, I'll write the info on the boards after you've noted it down from the files."

Logan nods and smiles, moving across the room to collect the pile of medical records and is surprised at the amount of information he will have to sift through. *Looks like some of these people have significant past medical histories, even if they do only go back a year!*

In a very large very cold house, there is an argument in progress.

"I couldn't do it. I won't do it," Helen states defiantly. "He's so young – who knows what medical breakthroughs there might be in the next few years. It isn't for certain that he'll never walk again!"

"I've told you before...it isn't up to you to choose who gains release. You heard the call, now follow its direction and do what you know you must," her mother insists firmly.

"Mother, please...," Helen implores, "...couldn't I give him just a little more time? He's due for more surgery that might change his prognosis for the better."

But her mother is adamant. "The chosen are selected for a reason – you do not possess the wisdom of God. It disappoints me that you would dare to think that you know better than the Lord God himself," her mother sighs and closes her eyes.

"But...I..." Feeling small and thoroughly chastised, Helen takes away the pots on the bedside table and walks towards the bedroom door. "I'm sorry, mother; of course I will do as the Lord God has decreed. I'm sorry to have disappointed you."

On the Orthopaedics ward the Matron is discussing the police investigation with the wards two Consultants and the Registrar.

"Apparently the police don't want us to make the investigation public knowledge," Sharon Findlay, the ward Matron, explains. "They asked for the off-duty for all staff that has patient contact – thank you for letting me have the medical off-duty, I've photocopied them and put them together with copies of our own off-duty," she tells Jason Mayberry.

Jason smiles and nods his acknowledgement. "Anything we can do to help, you only need to ask," he assures her. "The sooner we find out exactly what's going on the better."

Sharon narrows her eyes as she regards the middle aged doctor. "Do you have any theories?"

"I'm sure we all have our theories, but I think it might be better to let things unfold a little more before we attempt to act on any of them," Jason advises.

"What about you, Charles...how do you think we should handle this?" Sharon asks the other Consultant sitting in on the meeting.

Charles Henry is a good few years younger than Jason Mayberry and often known for his outspokenness - but in this instance he agrees with Jason. "With a great deal of caution...I think you're right, Jason," he turns towards his colleague, "we need to know more about what the police think has been going on before we start speculating."

"Did they not explain what they're investigating?" Raymond Forrester, the ward's senior Registrar asks. "I mean, don't they have to tell us why they want to look at our off-duty...you know...confidentiality and all that?"

But Sharon shakes her head, "Apparently they've discussed the issue with the powers that be and they've instructed us to comply with whatever the police ask of us."

"But...without any idea of what is wrong, how can we

guard against it happening again?" Raymond persists, his frown showing his impatience with the situation. "Did management not indicate whether we are looking at some form of theft or some sort of misconduct..."

But Sharon is already shaking her head. "Management have said that the investigation is extremely serious and that we will be apprised of the details as soon as the police give them the go ahead to do so."

"Well, that doesn't give us much to work with but what we do know is that something very serious has been happening right under our noses," Jason comments quietly. "So, what I suggest is we start documenting any suspicious behaviour and monitoring all staff as closely as possible without being obvious. And that goes for each other, too."

But Charles raises a brow and begins shaking his head, not in disagreement but rather in confusion.

"And how do we do that without being obvious? There are numerous staff on the ward each day going about a myriad duties – are we to follow them into the drug room to make sure they're not pocketing the stock or into the side-rooms to make sure they're not abusing a patient?" Lifting his hands and letting them fall into his lap in a gesture of despair, Charles again shakes his head. "Without any idea of what we're looking for we'll be chasing our tails and be too distracted to do our own jobs properly."

"I'm not suggesting that we start following the staff around...," Jason frowns sternly, "...only that we take the time to be more observant of what is going on around us and documenting anything suspicious!"

Before an argument can ensue, Sharon interjects, "I think that's the least we can do. We'll all have to be present on the ward more often than is usual but try to do so without making our presence felt."

"And how do you suggest we do that?" Raymond asks.

"By not drawing attention to ourselves," Sharon narrows her eyes at the young Registrar. "I will do more clinical work in the guise of updating my skills. I suggest you find similar excuses for having more of a presence on the ward!"

Eventually the meeting comes to an unsatisfactory end. They are all filled with concern but feel useless to act on it without the necessary information to enable them.

And so a shadow hangs over the ward, silent yet penetrating, all of the staff aware that 'something' is amiss.

CHAPTER TEN

Lying in Logan's arms, Catherine feels warm and safe, her world more perfect than she'd ever dreamed it could be.

"I spoke with Henry last night," she murmurs softly. "He said the builders are making great inroads into the project – says they reckon another couple of months should do it."

"Hmm, I might see if they'd be willing to up the pace...," Logan muses, his hand lazily trailing up and down her arm, "...maybe work in shifts to get it done as quickly as possible."

With a chuckle, Catherine kisses his chest and snuggles closer.

"You really are eager to move back home," she smiles into him.

"Yes. Now the decision has been made it's frustrating to have to wait," he tells her. "Plus it will mean the boys getting used to life here then having to adjust to a new nursery."

"Did it all arrive...," Catherine asks sleepily, "...the nursery stuff that Caroline picked out?"

Logan gives a low chuckle. "Come on...," he takes his arm from under her head and rolls out of bed, then flips the duvet off of her.

"What the hell!"

But Logan just laughs at her desperate efforts to drag the duvet back up the bed. Instead he flings her warm dressing-gown over her and tells her to get up.

"I've got something to show you," he smiles.

"Well, hell!"

Fighting her way into her dressing gown, Catherine is not at all happy.

Damn it! I was enjoying being snuggled up warm with my husband. Now he's got me all turned around and annoyed as hell...this had better be worth it!

Logan tries hard not to laugh as she finally stands, hair all a mess with her protrudent belly sticking out of the lopsided dressing gown.

Taking the edges of the fluffy dressing gown, Logan pulls her towards him and leans over her bump to kiss her pouting lips.

"Only you could look beautiful wearing an angry frown like that," he smiles. "Now come with me and I promise to replace it with a smile."

Leading her along the landing he opens the door of the bedroom next to their own and Catherine steps inside.

A hand flies up to cover her mouth, tears welling immediately in her wide blue eyes.

"This...is...beautiful," she whispers as she glides a hand over the first cot and then its twin not two feet away from it. *My boys have got a nursery...a beautiful nursery. Oh...they have a teddy bear in their cot to keep them company at night. And they have the same little sleeping bags...and...oh my lord, they even have their names on.*

"Logan, this is amazing...just..."

But Catherine can't manage any more words as tears begin to fall thick and fast.

Drawing her into his arms, Logan rests his cheek on the top of Catherine's head as her body shakes with her sobs. *You hide your emotions away deep inside like a dirty little secret most of the time, so when you let them out they swamp you. My beautiful, angry, taciturn woman...my heart aches for you.*

Wiping her eyes on the back of her sleeve, Catherine looks up at Logan with red rimmed eyes.

"How did you do this? When did you do this?" she asks, her bottom lip still quivering.

"Actually, I must confess, I had very little to do with any of it," Logan explains. "My job was just to keep you busy in the office to make sure you didn't come out and ruin the surprise. It was Caroline, Travis and Mrs Baines who did all the setting up."

"So that's what you were doing in my office yesterday," she realises, jabbing an accusatory finger into his chest.

"Guilty," he smiles. "But you can't complain – we got all that background information put up on the boards and you got a beautiful nursery for our boys."

Shaking her head, Catherine can only wonder at the great good fortune that had brought her this man.

"I'm not complaining," she tells him, her hand gently cupping his cheek. "I'm thanking my lucky stars that you came into my life...I love you more than I can ever tell you."

Logan is just about to reciprocate the sentiment when he notices her eyes go wide and a hand grasp at her stomach.

"What?! Catherine, was that a kick or a pain?" he asks desperately, guiding her to the rocking chair placed between the two cots.

"I...I don't know," she frowns, her face a picture of confusion. "I mean...it definitely wasn't a kick...but..."

And then it came again but Catherine still isn't sure what's going on.

"Catherine, you're scaring the hell out of me," Logan tells her, and she can actually see the fear in his watchful brown eyes.

"I don't know what's happening – I feel a pain but it isn't real," she tries to explain, then her eyes fly open wide as sudden dawning strikes.

"It's Caroline...she's gone into labour!"

But Logan isn't convinced. "I'm going to get Mrs Baines – you just sit there until we get back," he warns.

Then Catherine finds herself alone and smiling as she takes in her lovely nursery.

"You'll have a lovely home," she croons to her boys, stroking her stomach lovingly. "And you'll have three little cousins to play with – you'll never be alone or scared, mummy's here."

Just then she hears Logan telling Mrs Baines to hurry and then they stop and stare as they take in her tranquil smile.

Rocking back and forth, Catherine looks up and her eyes are bright with tears again.

"Isn't he wonderful," she asks Mrs Baines. "He did all

this without me suspecting a thing. And you helped...thank you so much."

"You're very welcome," the housekeeper tells her, moving to stand in front of Catherine. "Logan tells me you've been getting some pains...is that right?"

"No...not really. But I must get dressed and go to Caroline...she's in labour," Catherine grins happily.

Mrs Baines frowns, her concern evident.

"Catherine, you may think you're only feeling Caroline's pains, but it could be that you're in labour yourself," the housekeeper tries to explain.

Chuckling lightly, Catherine stands and her face lights up with the excitement she feels.

"Come on, I want to be with Caroline when she gives birth," Catherine states, moving past Logan and Mrs Baines to go to her bedroom.

"Well...I've never had dealings with twins, but it's possible that Catherine is right," Mrs Baines lets out a long sigh. "I mean, she doesn't look uncomfortable – it's like she's experiencing a shadow of the real pain, certainly nothing as intense as the onset of labour would be."

But Logan doesn't look convinced. "The only thing I can think is, thank God Caroline will be going to the hospital. At least Catherine will be in the right place if she has started labour!"

Mrs Baines grins, "Better take her things with you just in case."

Then Logan looks around the lovely nursery and suddenly the panic subsides.

"Our boys will be here soon...," he tells no one in particular, "...Adam and Andrew, our children." And he looks from one cot to the other imagining them there.

"Come on...," Catherine shouts as she makes her way down the stairs, "...we need to get over to Caroline's now! I'll phone Adrianne and dad in the car on the way!"

By the time they reach The Lovett Hotel, Catherine is certain that Caroline is progressing quickly. Stopping by the reception desk she asks the young woman sat behind it if she's called an ambulance.

"I...I...who for?" the poor startled girl asks.

"For Mrs Lovett, of course," Catherine frowns fiercely. "My sister is in labour and she's having twins – get an ambulance here right now!"

But Logan steps forward holding up a staying hand. "Let's not get ahead of ourselves. Just ring up to the penthouse and confirm Mrs Lovett's status, then we'll see what's what."

"Yes sir," the receptionist agrees, and picks up the telephone to do his bidding. But it doesn't take a mind reader to see that Catherine is right. "Yes Mr Travis, I'll call the ambulance right away!"

Looking up at Logan, Catherine gives him a smug smile. "What did I tell you – it isn't me, it's Caroline."

But Logan is just happy that in supporting Caroline, Catherine too will be in the maternity hospital.

Just then they hear Travis telling Caroline to take her time. "Please, let me help you," he tells her, taking Caroline's arm and steering her towards a comfy chair.

"Hey, are you ok?" Catherine asks as she crosses the foyer to her sister.

But Caroline doesn't look ok and is shaking her head. "I'm terrified," she wails quietly. "I know I've been impatient for this to happen but now that it's started I just want it to stop!"

Catherine puts a hand to her stomach and smiles at her sister, "You've got another one coming."

And sure enough, Caroline cringes as another contraction hits. Breathing through the pain, she keeps her eyes on Catherine, trying to calm herself.

"How the hell did you know that?!" Caroline gasps as the pain gradually fades.

"The same way you knew I was feeling sad the other day," Catherine tells her. "I thought it was me for a start, then I realised it wasn't and I knew you had gone in to labour."

"Oh god, Catherine, I don't want to do this – it's just

happening and I don't have any control," Caroline wails frantically.

"Just think of your girls...," Catherine soothes, "...very soon you'll be holding them in your arms and I'll be jealous as hell."

"Yes...I will won't I," she smiles a little more calm. "I never realised I was frightened of all this until it started to take over me and I knew there was no going back." Taking Catherine's hand she asks, "Will you stay with me, at the hospital, will you just be with me to the end?"

Looking up at Travis, Catherine silently asks his permission and receives a happy smile and a nod of assent.

Truth be known, he is glad of the support himself. When Caroline had told him that she was having contractions all the blood had seemed to drain out of him.

"Alright, but you have to return the favour," Catherine tells her twin. "I phoned dad and Adrianne on the way over, they should be here soon."

Just then a couple of burly ambulance men came into the foyer and were directed to where the twins are sitting.

At first they give a comical gasp of surprise, then one of them asks, "Are you both in labour?"

But Catherine chuckles and shakes her head. "Just one

of us. My sister has beaten me to it."

"Alright, my lovely...," the taller of the two men crouches down in front of Caroline, "...it's up to you whether you walk to the ambulance or we can get you into this seat and we'll wheel you out."

Then another contraction hits and Caroline lets out a small moan as she tries to breathe through it.

"If you don't mind, I think I'll take you up on your offer to wheel me out," she smiles wanly when the pain subsides. "I'm so scared I don't think my legs will carry me."

The two men help Caroline to her feet and continue to offer support while she makes her way to the chair and is then safely seated.

"That's the way...I'm just going to tilt the chair back now and we'll have you in the ambulance in a jiffy," the strapping ambulance man tells her.

And sure enough, seconds later they are speeding away to the hospital with Catherine and Logan following behind in the Range Rover.

"I ought to phone Adrianne and dad," Catherine says while she rummages through her bag for her mobile. "They'll turn up at the hotel and wonder what's going on."

"I'm sure reception will redirect them to the hospital," Logan assures her, feeling much calmer now that he knows it really isn't Catherine that has gone into labour.

Unable to find her mobile, Catherine gives up. "Ok, I can't find my darn mobile anyway. I bet I left it in the bedroom, we did leave in a bit of a hurry."

"Stop worrying, they'll be fine," Logan tells her as they pull up at the hospital behind the ambulance. "You get out here and go with Caroline; I'll park the car over there and be back in a sec'."

"The contractions are getting closer together," the ambulance man tells the midwife who has come to meet them. Then they all watch as Caroline gets another contraction and Catherine holds her stomach as she feels it clench her own womb. "They seem to be in some kind of sync – this is the one in labour but her twin seems to feel every contraction," he explains, scratching his thatch of hair.

"Well, ladies, I'm Suzie and I'm going to be looking after you," she smiles brightly. "Let's get you up to the labour suite. Are you the father...or..." her eyes turn from Travis to Logan who has just entered the main doors.

"That would be him...," Catherine points to Travis, "...he's mine."

With a handsome smile Logan comes to stand by his wife, proud to have been claimed.

"How are we doing?" he asks both girls.

"She's getting another contraction...," Catherine states with a hand to her belly, then her smile slips and a frown creases her brow. "That must have been a doozy, I really felt that!"

The midwife looks at Catherine with narrowed eyes. Turning to the ambulance man she says, "Do you happen to have a wheelchair with you – I only brought the one down," and she nods her head towards Catherine to indicate the problem.

"Oh!" he breathes, realising what the midwife means. "We could use the tilt-back – I'll come up with you. It'll save you calling up for someone to come and help you."

Minutes later they are all in the homely labour suite, Caroline is settled on the bed and Travis is sat beside it holding her hand.

Another midwife enters the room and eyes Catherine speculatively.

"Hi, I'm Aimee...," she smiles warmly, "...would you mind if I just take a look at you, just to be on the safe side?"

Frowning, Catherine shakes her head, "I'm fine, it's her that's in labour – I'm just feeling her pain," she shrugs.

"Never the less...," Aimee insists, "...it would set my mind at rest if we could just make sure."

Rolling her eyes at Logan, Catherine turns to Caroline

and says, "I'll be back in a minute."

"Don't be long, these contractions are getting closer than ever," Caroline tells her anxiously.

"Don't worry, we're only going to the room next door," Aimee assures her.

"I'm fine...," Catherine sighs as she climbs up on the bed and makes herself comfortable, "...we just feel each other's feelings. Though that last one was a bit sharper than the rest," she frowns up at Logan who now comes to sit at the side of the bed, just as Travis is with Caroline.

"We'll go back in the minute you're finished," Logan states, taking her hand and giving it a gentle squeeze.

But when the midwife examines her she is shocked to find that Catherine is already in established labour. "I'm afraid you won't be going back in with your sister – you're 4 cm dilated."

"W...what the hell does that mean?" Catherine turns to Logan in stunned disbelief.

Looking just as stunned, Logan gives an uncertain laugh, "I think it means the boys want out!"

"The...no...no...I'm not ready for this, I only came in with Caroline...I am not ready to have the boys yet!" she panics, and tries to sit up to climb off the bed. But Logan is too quick for her.

"Be a good girl and do as Aimee tells you," he instructs

firmly. "I'm right here; I won't leave you, not even for a minute."

Grabbing his hand, Catherine holds on for dear life and stares Logan straight in the eyes. "I can't do this...I'm not a mother...I'm a freak who swears like a trouper and hates everyone. You get it!"

But Logan just smiles and shakes his head ignoring her use of the 'f' word, "You are the kindest, most loving woman it has been my pleasure to meet. And you don't swear any more...remember?!"

Flopping back on the bed as a contraction hits, Catherine keeps hold of Logan's hand and grits her teeth as she feels the full force of it.

"Damn it, Logan!

Aimee, the midwife, comes to the side of the bed and strokes her brow, "Do you remember about gas and air?" And when Catherine grimaces a silent nod she says, "You can start using it now, if you feel you need to take the edge off the pain."

But still gritting her teeth, Catherine shakes her head, focusing on Logan and drawing strength from the certainty of his love.

"I'm right here," he kisses her white knuckles.

"Caroline..." she gasps, then closes her eyes as the pain subsides once more. "Is she alright?"

"Caroline is doing well...," Aimee tells her, "...I had my student go check on her and she's coping well."

"But I said I'd stay with her," Catherine pants.

"She knows that you're in labour too and seemed strangely comforted by that fact," Aimee chuckles, remembering her student's recounting of Caroline's exact words.

But she doesn't need to tell Catherine for her to get the gist. "I'll bet she was," and actually manages a laugh. "Is Travis holding up ok?"

"He's being very supportive," and Aimee grins at her student.

The student's cheeks pink up when Catherine frowns at her, but when she just laughs the student relaxes. "I'll bet he's learning a whole new vocabulary while he's at it!"

Understanding her meaning, Aimee laughs and nods, "Apparently he keeps apologising and assuring everyone that his wife doesn't usually swear like that."

"That's true," Catherine nods, then grimaces when another contraction starts to build.

The contractions are getting much closer together and lasting longer – Catherine barely gets time to rest in between.

For five hours Catherine and Logan battle the physical and emotional struggle to bring their boys into the world.

When her 'waters' break, Catherine is startled yet relieved.

"That's good, isn't it?" Catherine asks, finding it difficult to remember everything now that she is in the thick of the action.

"Yes...," Aimee tells her as she watches the monitor that shows the babies' heart beats, "...you're progressing well and the boys appear to be happy enough."

"You get them out if there's any sign of them struggling, right," Catherine states emphatically.

"No problem, Catherine – we have your birth plan right here and your consent for a caesarean should it become necessary," Aimee smiles.

After another hour of watching his wife deal with the pain of contractions, Logan grows concerned.

"You're exhausted, Catherine...," he smiles as he strokes the hair back from her sweaty brow, "...wouldn't it be better to opt for the caesarean now?"

"No. I can do this," Catherine squeezes the hand that she's been wringing like an old dishcloth.

"Then at least use the gas and air," he encourages, but isn't surprised when she stubbornly shakes her head.

"I don't want any drugs, not even gas and air," she asserts firmly. "I won't put our boys at risk by not being fully alert and ready. I can do this," Catherine reiterates, her eyes pleading with Logan to support her decision.

"Of course you can," he smiles proudly. "I'm just being a wimp on your behalf. I hate to see you suffer like this."

"I'd like to ask your Obstetrician to come in and take a look at you," Aimee tells Catherine when her contraction starts to ease. "You're almost 10 cm dilated; it's getting close to the time when we'll need you to push."

"Ok, whatever you think," Catherine agrees. "You won't forget the zygosity testing when the twins are born," she reminds Aimee about what they had discussed on her birth plan. "We want to know if the twins are identical or not."

"We're all ready for that," the young midwife assures her. Then turning to her student she asks, "Would you asks Mrs Payne to come in please."

"What a name – I hope she isn't into inflicting it," Catherine grimaces as the student goes out.

"You met at one of your consultations, didn't you?" Aimee asks.

"Yes, but it only just struck me about her name."

The door opens and a woman in her late 30s enters the labour suite.

"Hello...," she greets first Catherine and then Logan, taking their hands in turn, "...I hear you're getting near to the second stage – would you mind if I take a look?"

"Help yourself...," Catherine agrees, "... let's just get this done!"

After a quiet chat with the midwife, Mrs Payne examines Catherine.

"Do you feel the need to push yet?" she asks after assessing the progress of the labour.

Nodding, Catherine looks over at Logan and says, "We're going to meet our boys. They're real!"

Chuckling softly, Logan kisses her lips and strokes back her hair. "They certainly are, and I can't wait to hold them."

Just then the need to push grew stronger. "Is it ok to push, I don't think I can stop myself much longer."

"Yes, push away and we'll guide you through it," Aimee tells her and moves to stand ready at the foot of the bed.

"Ok, relax and breathe," Mrs Payne encourages. "You need to save your strength and take in some much needed oxygen while you can."

"You're crowning," the student gasps in amazement.

"That's the head, right?" Catherine frowns.

"It is indeed," Aimee smiles.

And then Catherine is pushing again while Logan helps to support her back off the bed.

After the fourth huge push Catherine is scared.

"I can't do it...I can't get them out!"

Another contraction grips her and Logan clasps her hand and supports her back as she leans up to put all her weight behind the next push.

The first baby to enter the world is proclaimed to be Andrew by his ecstatic mother. Ten minutes later Adam is born and their family is finally complete.

"You wonderful, wonderful woman!" Logan hugs Catherine and the boys as they lay on her naked chest and open their lungs in protest.

CHAPTER ELEVEN

Mrs Baines is beaming down at the baby in her arms. "There, there, your mummy will get to you in just a minute," she croons to Adam as Catherine settles his brother onto her breast.

"Ok...I think I'm ready," Catherine looks up.

Positioning the baby in Catherine's other arm, the two boys are soon suckling contentedly.

"I should feel like a cow, but somehow I don't," Catherine smiles down at her boys, snuggled into her body as nature intended.

"Even if you only manage a week or two of breast feeding, you will have given your boys the very best start," the housekeeper smiles.

Catherine rocks in her chair, enjoying this moment of bonding with her babies.

When Logan walks into the nursery he finds her looking serene and perfectly at ease.

"And you didn't think you would make a very good mother," he shakes his head and pulls up a chair to sit with his new family. "You're a natural; don't you agree Mrs Baines?"

"I certainly do. You've been home less than a week and already you've got a good routine going," the housekeeper says approvingly.

"Only with your help," Catherine smiles up shyly. "I'm so glad you're here – I would have been scared to death without you."

"I'm glad to help," Mrs Baines tells her proudly.

"And you really didn't mind leaving your cottage?" Catherine asks for the umpteenth time.

"Not a bit," Mrs Baines smiles. "I think the thought of leaving it behind was worse than the actual doing. Now it's done I'm quite content to devote my time to you and the boys."

"Then can we please drop the formalities?" Catherine asks, and looks to Logan for support.

Nodding, Logan looks to his housekeeper and says, "With your permission we'd like to adopt you as Adam and Andrew's grandmother and, as such, we'd like to use your Christian name from now on?"

Mrs Baines looks thrilled and embarrassed all at once and her kindly eyes fill with tears. "I...I don't know what to say."

"Just say yes," Catherine suggests with a smile.

And the housekeeper takes pleasure in doing as she's told. "Yes. I never thought I'd be a grandmother, this is such an honour."

"Ha...," Catherine laughs, "...you do know that grandmothers get to do babysitting duties and changing pooey nappies!"

"It will be my pleasure," the housekeeper beams, wiping her eyes on her apron.

"So what do we call you now?" Catherine asks.

"Well...my name is Belinda, but if you wouldn't mind, I prefer Linda."

"Belinda is a lovely name, but if you prefer Linda then Linda it is," Logan nods and smiles happily.

"Well...I'll just go make some tea," Linda excuses herself, overcome with emotion.

"I think we just made her cry," Catherine looks at Logan, her blue eyes filled with concern.

"Don't worry, they're happy tears," Logan assures her, his pride in his wife written all over his handsome face.

"Ok, if you say so," she smiles, and just then Adam decides he's had enough milk and lets go of her nipple.

"Here, you take Adam while I finish off with Andrew – but get a muslin first," and she points to a pile of folded cloths on the baby changing table. "He'll need winding and he always brings up some feed while he's at it."

Having watched Catherine do it previously, Logan holds the muslin under Adam's chin while he gently pats his son's back.

Moments later a small fountain of milk is expelled along with a loud burp.

"Told you," Catherine chuckles as she straightens her clothing and prepares to wind Andrew. "This one isn't so greedy; he seems to take just what he needs and doesn't vomit so much."

Adam is already falling asleep in his daddy's arms but Logan is loath to put him down in his cot.

"I know I've told you this a thousand times...but...," looking adoringly at Catherine, Logan tries to put his feelings into words, "...I love you and our boys so much. You've made me the happiest man on the planet."

Cuddling Andrew to her, Catherine smiles shyly, still not comfortable around emotional declarations.

"You know I love you too, right? Even though I don't say it a lot," and she buries her head into her son as a distraction.

"I know," Logan reaches out to stroke her hair.

"I wonder if Emma's here?" Catherine asks, changing the subject none too subtly.

"Ah, yes, you're starting back to work today," he frowns, concerned that Catherine might be rushing into things. "Are you sure you wouldn't like to give it another couple of days – you're not getting a full night's sleep yet, even with me and Mrs...I mean Linda helping out with night feeds."

Chuckling, Catherine stands and lays Andrew in his cot then takes Adam from his father and lays him down too.

"It's going to take a while to get used to calling her that," she straightens and puts her arms around Logan's neck. "But it feels nice that our boys have a grandma – and I think Linda will be wonderful."

"And you...," Logan kisses her upturned lips and hugs her to him, "...will you be alright going back to work so soon?"

"I'm chomping at the bit," Catherine wiggles her eyebrows comically. "You know me, I can't sit still for long and my brain needs a workout."

Knowing how frustrated Catherine can get if she isn't stretching herself, Logan just smiles and agrees.

"Ok, wife, go and get ready while I sit with our boys for a while," and taking a seat in the rocking chair he watches her quick exit then turns his head from one side to the other, watching his sons sleep peacefully.

When Emma arrives she is all fired up for the day ahead. After giving Catherine a hug of greeting she asks after the twins. "Can I take a peek?"

Feeling awkward for being so proud of her boys, Catherine automatically shakes her head and moves out of Emma's reach.

"We need to get some work done," she states with an embarrassed frown. "You already saw the boys, they haven't changed that much in a few days," she insists, though she knows that isn't true.

Both Adam and Andrew have changed so much since the day they were born. They're already showing individual characteristics; like the way Andrew likes to snuggle into his mother, whereas Adam likes to be held more loosely and seems to have taken more to his dad.

Well he likes me well enough when it's time for his feed. And he looks happy, or at least contented, when I'm changing his nappy – so I must be doing something right.

But Emma isn't taking no for an answer. "Oh please. Please, please, please, please, please," she begs pitifully.

"Oh alright," Catherine frowns, though she isn't really annoyed. "Doesn't look like I'm going to get any peace until you do!"

Standing quietly at the foot of the cots, Emma and

Catherine smile at each other as they come across Logan fast asleep in the rocking chair.

"He and Linda took the night shift to give me some sleep," Catherine whispers.

Emma coos over the babies, fast asleep in their cots, and has to restrain herself from reaching out to stroke their hair in case she wakes them.

Back in their office the girls chuckle softly.

"Poor Logan, he really looked out of it," Emma laughs as she crosses to the kettle. "You fancy a coffee?"

Nodding, Catherine goes to her desk and fires up her laptop. "You need to bring me up to date with where we are in the investigation."

"Sure," Emma says as she spoons coffee into mugs. After pouring boiling water into them she gives a mug to Catherine and takes her own over to her desk. "I didn't realise you were planning to get a nanny...," Emma observes as she turns on her laptop.

"What...?"

"A nanny – I didn't realise you were going to have one," Emma looks over at Catherine.

"I haven't," Catherine frowns in confusion.

"Then...who's Linda?" Emma asks, equally confused.

Rolling her eyes at herself, Catherine explains. "We asked Mrs Baines to be Adam and Andrew's adopted grandmother, and she agreed. We can hardly keep calling our son's grandmother Mrs Baines."

"That's lovely," Emma smiles brightly. "She'll make a wonderful grandmother."

Nodding, Catherine agrees, "Yes, she's great with the boys, and I'm not as scared around them knowing that Linda is here and willing to help. I was terrified of trying to cope on my own."

"I'd be the same," Emma admits. "Even one baby would be daunting, but two..."

"Right...well, what about that update you're supposed to be giving me," Catherine asks, snapping back into work mode.

Taking out a small bunch of paperwork, Emma begins using the magnets to pin some of them to the white boards.

"As well as continuing our search for more possible victims from years ago, I've been keeping an eye on recent deaths...," Emma explains. "...those that have occurred since my aunt's death when we first started looking into this."

"Looks like you found some," Catherine sighs.

"Actually, just one...but it's a shocker," Emma tells her, her brow creasing in concern. "If I'm correct our perp just escalated big time. Timothy Givens was just 23 years old, he was in the hospital due to a motorcycle crash that smashed him up pretty badly – it was less than 50:50 that he would ever walk again," Emma sighs heavily.

"And you think he was taken out by our perp...why?" Catherine turns sceptical eyes to her partner.

"Because he had undergone surgery and the prognosis had been surprisingly optimistic," Emma explains. "Apparently they found that his spine was not as badly damaged as was first thought – some nerve damage was evident, but they relieved pressure on others that gave them a small hope of his regaining some use of his legs."

"That all sounds good, but you still haven't said why you think he might be a victim," Catherine persists.

"According to his records, everything was looking on the up and up – he is another patient that was expected to do well," Emma closes her eyes on a sigh then turns to Catherine. "The doctors have noted in his medical records that his death is suspicious and as such has immediately been referred to the Coroner."

"Fuck!" Catherine explodes, then a hand flies up to cover her mouth and her eyes go wide while her other hand moves to her stomach. *Thank Christ for that! I need to get a grip; I don't want our boys hearing me swear like that!*

"Sorry," she tells Emma awkwardly. "I guess it was just

such a shock. What's all that paperwork you have there?"

"I printed off his last year of medical records – like we did for the others," Emma clarifies. "I'll write the synopsis up on the board."

"Have you discussed this with Shivers?"

"Yes, of course," Emma sounds defensive but holds her ground. "I had to bounce the idea off someone and you were a bit preoccupied at the time."

"I'm not complaining," Catherine holds up her hands in surrender. "I just wanted to know if they were aware of this latest development, and what they thought it might mean."

"Actually, Sloane knows that we're starting back work in the office today and asked if they could come by to discuss our findings later this afternoon," Emma tells her warily, knowing that Catherine is not enamoured of her detective boyfriend.

"Great! We need to get on top of this – that's a massive escalation," Catherine worries her bottom lip while striding back and forth in front of the boards. "Now we need to be on the lookout for any age, sex or illness type – this monster just went right off the rails!"

When Inspector Frank Harper and Detective Sloane Shivers arrive later that afternoon, both women are anxious to get their expert input."

Catherine barely bothers with the formalities of greeting the men and dives right in with her questions.

"Is this for real? I mean, is it likely that the perp would go so far off their original track?" she asks almost praying for them to say not.

But Frank and Sloane both nod their heads, and while Frank discusses the case Sloane takes a look at the information they've put up on the boards.

"I'm afraid this is nothing less than we have been expecting," Frank sighs heavily. "The shortening of the time between victims was a sure indicator that the perpetrator was escalating — unfortunately we haven't narrowed down that list you gave us as yet."

"Cancer!" Sloane suddenly pronounces. "That's the connection."

Moving to stand next to him, Emma looks from one past medical history to another but shakes her head. "No, I'm not so sure. Only a couple of these were still undergoing treatment. Some have been in remission for a number of years and a couple are beyond hope of treatment." Turning to Sloane she says, "If it were the cancer wouldn't they be targeting the terminally ill ones — sort of...putting them out of their misery, if that's what they're doing?"

"If you look at the earlier victims, that appears to be

correct," Sloane agrees. "I think relieving their suffering may have been the goal in the beginning – but as the perp escalated they targeted anyone with cancer, dying or not, and the time between kills shortened!"

"Jesus...," Catherine sighs, "...you're right."

"But what about Tim, the latest victim – he didn't have any history of cancer," Emma states, unconvinced.

But Catherine steps in before Sloane or Frank can answer. "As far as the perp is concerned, what Tim was suffering was just as bad. You said yourself that it was a big possibility that he would never walk again – maybe our perp thinks it's better to be dead than in a wheelchair?"

Looking wide eyed and indignant, Emma rounds on Catherine, "But that's ridiculous. Tim might have had a good quality of life, wheelchair bound or not!"

"I didn't say that's what I believe," Catherine states calmly. "But I do think it might be the rationale the perp used for justifying the kill in their minds."

"I agree," Sloane surprises everyone. "From now on the perp isn't just looking for immediate suffering, they're determining the quality of life the patient has and if it doesn't meet the perp's idea of acceptable, that will be enough of a reason to kill them – to end their misery."

Suddenly, Emma tears up and struggles to hold them

back, "This is wrong on so many levels. Izzy fought and won against cancer, then some crazy person judges her life not worth living. They had no right! No damned right!"

Moving instinctively, Sloane pulls her into his arms and ignores the other people in the room. "We'll stop them, Em'," he comforts her. "Between us we'll put a stop to this monster!"

Lifting a brow at Sloane's implied acceptance of what they do, Catherine watches the embrace curiously.

It isn't that she is embarrassed by it, but she hasn't grown up around love and seeing it so openly and easily expressed is...

"Alright, knock it off...," she tells them suddenly, "...we need to get back to work and catch the bad guy, remember?"

Drawing apart, Sloane cups Emma's cheek and draws his thumb across it to wipe away a stray tear.

"You ok?" he asks, his grey eyes full of concern.

Nodding, Emma pulls her emotions in and turns back to the boards. "I'm ready. Let's get down to work and find the bastard!"

Instinctively Catherine's hands fly to her stomach, but her boys are safely tucked up in the nursery down the hall.

When will I get used to not having them inside me? I

thought I'd be glad to get them out...but somehow I'm not. I miss feeling them move, knowing they're safe. It's a whole lot scarier having them on the outside!

But then Catherine remembers how it feels to breastfeed her boys and smiles.

Scarier, but wonderful! I didn't know I had this much love inside me. Sometimes I feel like I could burst with it...but it's scary at the same time. I'd kill anyone that tried to harm them...and I'd make them pay!

CHAPTER TWELVE

Later that evening, after a gruelling afternoon working with the two detectives and her partner, Emma, Catherine is in the nursery feeding her boys.

When Logan comes upon them he is filled with love and pride and...

I know what Catherine means now when she says that love can be frightening. My world is sitting in that rocking chair...I don't know how I'd go on without them.

And then he remembers his dad and how he suffered when his mother died so suddenly.

I thought I understood, thought I had felt her loss just as deeply...but this kind of love is soul deep!

"You look so lovely," he tells Catherine, bringing up a chair to sit with them. Reaching out a hand he gently stokes the back of his fingers up and down her soft cheek.

"I can't get over the miracle of our boys, of our family. And I never knew that love could be so painful," he frowns, then smiles when he sees Catherine nod enthusiastically.

"I thought it was just me being me," she gasps, her eyes going wide with wonder. "I mean, I only just got used to how I feel about you, the way love seems to swamp me when you walk in a room," she tells him, not realising how much she has made his heart swell. "Now I'm swamped by so much love it really does feel painful, and I'm so scared of losing it. Of losing you and the boys," and quite unexpectedly Catherine bursts into tears.

Now Logan's hand moves to cup her cheek and Catherine lays her head against it.

"I won't pretend I don't understand," Logan tells her. "Losing your mother the way you did, it's only natural that you would be frightened of even more loss. But I won't let anyone harm my family – I'd do anything to keep you and the boys safe!"

Nodding, Catherine gives a pitiful sniff then turns her face into his palm and kisses it.

"I had the same thought this afternoon," she admits. "It suddenly hit me that I miss having the boys with me all the time, safe inside me. And I thought about what I'd do if anyone tried to harm them and I swear, I'd kill them as soon as look at them...and I'd take my time about it too!"

"A scary thought...," Logan chuckles, lightening the mood, "...but I'd be right there with you."

"Good to know," Catherine also chuckles, but hugs her boys to her breasts wanting to feel them safe in her arms.

"How did you get on this afternoon?" Logan asks, knowing that Catherine and Sloane Shivers are not the best of friends. "Did you and Shivers come to blows?" he jokes, but only just.

"Actually...," Catherine frowns, musing over her feelings about the brash detective, "...I think he's growing on me. At least, he's not the complete jerk I thought he was."

"Should I be worried," Logan chuckles again.

"No! Didn't I just get through telling you how much I love you," Catherine overreacts.

"I was joking," Logan reaches out to touch her cheek again with gentle fingers. "It was wrong of me, but I couldn't resist. It is something of a turnaround for you, though. I thought you couldn't stand the man?"

"I'm not saying I want to be his best buddy," Catherine states flatly as she hands Andrew to Logan and sits Adam up on her knee to pat his back, watching as Logan does the same with Andrew. "But I have seen another side to him. He cares about Emma."

Logan just lifts a brow, to him that much had been obvious from day one.

"No, I mean, he really cares about her," she emphasises. "When she got upset this afternoon, he hugged her...right in front of me and Frank, like he'd forgotten that we were in the room."

Feeling sad that such displays of affection only seem to confuse Catherine, Logan has to remind himself of the life she had lead before he met her.

"I'm glad they seem to be working things out. Didn't you say they hit a rocky patch a while back?"

Nodding, Catherine moves to the changing table to put a fresh nappy on Adam. "I think it was mostly caused by the death of Emma's aunt. She was really close with her and her death hit her badly."

Then Catherine hands Adam to Logan and takes Andrew from him to change his nappy too. "Of course, it didn't help that Shivers can be a jerk at times, but Emma couldn't talk about her aunt's death at first and he said some things he probably wouldn't have if he'd known about it."

Distracted by their conversation, Catherine cries out in shock when Andrew does a wee that fountains up and over her and everything around them.

"Bloody hell!" she screams, her hands trying to stop

the spurt of urine from drenching her, while Logan rocks with laughter.

"That was not funny!" she tells him as she cleans Andrew up and quickly gets a nappy on him.

But Logan is unrepentant. "Oh yes it was," he laughs and rocks with Adam lying contentedly over his shoulder. Then he sees her lips tremble into a reluctant smile. "It really was."

"Well let's see how you manage...," she smirks, bringing Andrew up to lie on her shoulder as his brother is on Logan's, "...it'll be your turn to change them next – then we'll see how funny it is."

But Catherine is not angry; in fact she is chuckling at the incident now that it's over.

"I'll be more prepared, having the same equipment," he smiles smugly.

They enjoy the feeling of the boys lying warm and happy on their mum and dad and rock in unison, unaware of the natural rhythm.

"I suppose we'd better put them down," Logan stands, but doesn't move to relinquish the hold he has on his son.

"I need a shower, otherwise I'd just sit and rock with them for a while," she says, eyeing the rocking chair longingly.

"I think I'll get another one," Logan tells her. "I think

I'd enjoy rocking the boys together."

"Good idea," she smiles, and her blue eyes fill with the bright light of love. "That would be nice."

When they move into the bedroom, minus the now sleeping boys, Catherine heads for the shower.

It makes her smile when she strips off the top that is still wet with Andrew's wee.

You little tinker...I won't make that mistake again. "Aahhh," she screams when Logan's arms come around her. "You idiot – you scared me half to death!"

But Logan just laughs and swallows any further protests with a long, lusty kiss.

"I've missed you woman," he croons into her ear, then he nibbles on the lobe and sends shivers quivering down her spine.

"You certainly have," she agrees, taking his hard length in her hand and massaging him gently. "And I've missed you too."

His hands begin a leisurely exploration of her body, her full breasts filling them handsomely.

"I wondered if I'd be jealous watching you breastfeed the boys...but I love seeing you so relaxed with them. And these...," he dips his head to taste first one and then the other, flicking the pebble-like nipple with his tongue, "...are even more tasty and adorable."

When a hand moves down her abdomen, circling over her bellybutton then furrowing between her legs, Catherine moves to accommodate him.

"Ohhh god..." Her head falls back and while pushing his long fingers into the heat of her, Logan's mouth tastes her neck and shoulders.

Her groans fuel his lust and his hardness becomes like rock. He doesn't just want her, he needs Catherine like a man who has been denied his fix of heroine.

Backing her up against the wall, Logan lifts her, his hands cupping her neat bottom as her legs wind around his waist.

She is as ready and as needy as he and Logan doesn't keep her waiting.

Sliding into her, Logan tries to be gentle, worrying that he might hurt Catherine as it's only a week since she gave birth to their twin boys.

But Catherine isn't having that! Once she has Logan inside her she holds his shoulders and moves her hips impatiently.

It doesn't take long for him to catch on that she needs more and takes great pleasure in giving it to her.

Their bodies are so in tune that they move in unison, their moans of joy building as their insides tense. The noise of their bodies slapping together echo in the large wet-room and only serves to drive them on, faster, harder, deeper.

"Catherine..." Logan's deep breathy groan is anything but reverent; it is guttural and claims her as his. "Now!" he demands, and only when he feels her body tremble on the edge of orgasm does he allow himself to fill her.

Their hearts are beating wildly, their arms and legs still wrapped around each other, and their love is fulfilled...for now.

Moving his hand to gently brush back her wet hair, Logan asks, "Are you alright...I don't want to hurt you," he tells her, then is shocked to feel her hips slowly rock against him.

"I've never been better...and if I'm not mistaken you're still hard!" and she chuckles sexily.

"And you're still horny," he smiles and wiggles his eyebrows making her laugh. And then his hips begin to move, slowly this time taking them up again in a drawn out rhythm that drives Catherine crazy.

Gripping her long legs tightly round his waist she grinds her groin against him and lets out a guttural groan that makes him chuckle momentarily.

"Is this what you want?" he asks, thrusting into her more forcefully and listens to her groans of pleasure as he continues to quicken the pace.

Her fingers are digging into Logan's thick muscled shoulders as Catherine gets nearer to falling apart in his arms.

"I love you," she cries out, then any more thoughts are lost as her breath comes in short gasps and her world tips on its axis for a second time.

"Christ, woman, you'll be the death of me," Logan groans into her neck, loving the feel of her jumping pulse under his lips.

"I began to wonder if you would ever come near me," Catherine tells him as she eventually slides down his wonderfully sculpted body.

"You've just given birth to twins," Logan reminds her. "Of course I've waited, but that doesn't mean that I haven't wanted to make love to you. It's been hell trying to keep my hands off you."

Heaving a long sigh of relief, Catherine goes up on tiptoes to give him a quick kiss.

"Good. I've heard that some men go off their wives once they become a mother. Something to do with the trauma of watching her give birth, I think," she frowns giving it some more thought.

"Well, I think we just proved that neither of us has gone off the other," he chuckles and moves to fill his palm with shower gel.

"Hmm...Logan, can we go and visit Caroline and Travis," Catherine asks, sounding distracted. "I've only spoken to her on the phone...it would be nice to meet the girls."

"That's a great idea. Why don't you catch up with Emma first and let her know that we're going to be gone for a couple of hours," he readily agrees. "I'll ask Mrs Baines...I mean, Linda, to watch Andrew and Adam and we'll be set."

During the drive over to see her sister, Catherine speculates about their impending move to Lakelands.

"Logan, when we move to Lakelands I will be able to come see my sisters, right?"

Glancing sideways, Logan sees that Catherine is biting her bottom lip and looks really worried.

"Of course. But...have you changed your mind about moving? Because if you have we can continue the build and just use it for extended visits."

"No. No. I haven't changed my mind," she assures him. "It's just...you don't seem to want me to drive and I can't ask you to just drop everything to bring me to see my sisters."

Letting out a relieved chuckle, Logan takes a hand off the steering wheel to pat her knee.

"I just jumped in the Range Rover out of habit," he

admits. "Now that you're not pregnant, there's no reason for you not to drive."

"Good." And her smile returns to full on relaxed.

With her independence back in place, Catherine begins to enjoy the thought of getting their moving schedule underway.

"Do you have any idea when we will be moving?" she asks, suddenly fired up with renewed enthusiasm. "I need to ask Caroline how far along she is with the refurbishments and Emma needs to make sure that the gatehouse is sorted – though she could use a bedroom in the main house for a while, couldn't she?" But Catherine doesn't give Logan time to answer any of her questions.

"We ought to go down to your dad's and check it out for ourselves – and we can take the boys," she grins happily. "They'll get to see their new home for the first time!"

As they pull in to the Lovett's car park, Logan brings the car to a stop then turns in his seat to face Catherine. He is smiling broadly and she looks at him perplexed.

"What?"

"No, not exactly, the refurbishment is going well, yes...that shouldn't be a problem and yes again, a visit would be great," Logan tells her and watches Catherine's brow crease in confusion.

"What the hell?!" she snaps irritably.

"I'm just answering all your questions in one go while I can get a word in edgeways," he laughs, putting a gentle hand to her cheek. "You're really excited about this?"

"Well...yes," she admits a little shyly. "We're moving home. It will be the very first complete family home I've ever had, or can remember anyway."

It tugs at Logan to hear her say it, yet he is also glad that he can give Catherine the one thing that it seems she has been longing for.

"You don't think of our present house as home?" he asks quietly.

Shaking her head, Catherine looks up through her long lashes cautiously. "I don't think you do either. Not really. You said it yourself; you just never seemed to get around to going home after uni'...that sounds like you've always thought of Lakelands as your real home," she observes quietly

Taking in a lung full of air, Logan lets it go on a long sigh. "You're right, of course. I just never realised it until I met you."

Unbuckling his seatbelt, Logan leans across to kiss her and says, "You are a very special woman and I'm looking forward to being with you at Lakelands."

Flinging her arms around his neck, Catherine hugs him

to her. "I love you, Logan Sayers."

Returning the hug, Logan replies, "I'm very glad to hear it!"

When the twins meet they can't stop hugging.

"I'm sorry...," Catherine tells her sister, feeling like she had let her down, "...I wanted to come back to you but they wouldn't let me."

"I shouldn't think so," Caroline tells her. "It was really quite encouraging to know that we were both going through it together."

Catherine pulls back and frowns at her sister. "Yeah, I remember someone saying that it cheered you up no end!"

Throwing her head back on a laugh, Caroline again pulls Catherine into a hug. "You idiot! It was just the connection – if you could do it then so could I!"

"Oh. Well...that's alright then." Catherine moves further into the large lounge and takes a seat with Logan on the settee. "So...do I get to meet my nieces or what?"

Beaming with pride, Caroline and Travis both disappear for a moment then come back with two tiny bundles wrapped in pink blankets.

Passing her bundle to Catherine, Caroline introduces the baby," This is Sara Patricia Lovett, and she's a very good girl for her mummy."

Then Travis hands his little bundle over to Logan with a broad, proud grin, "And this little lady is Leanne Camille Lovett; she seems to like exercising her lungs a bit more than her sister."

Leaning over, Catherine takes a peek at Leanne and back to the baby in her arms. "They look identical, are you having the test done to confirm it?"

"Yes. Though I'm not really bothered either way," she admits. "I'd just like to know for sure."

"Hmm, me too," Catherine agrees. "As long as they're fine and healthy I'm happy."

"Have you seen Adrianne lately – I saw her on the day I came home with the girls but I haven't heard from her since?" Caroline asks with a concerned frown.

"I spoke to her last night, she's ok but a bit grouchy," Catherine recalls. "I think she's a bit jealous that we got it over with and she's still waiting."

Raising her brows, Caroline gives a chuckle. "I sort of remember thinking the same thing, but when it started I would have given anything to be able to stop it from happening. I was terrified!"

Not answering right away, Catherine looks at Logan and a smile tugs at her lips. "I wasn't that worried by the labour itself – I was more afraid of becoming a mother. I just knew I wouldn't be any good at it." But when she sees

Logan's frown she adds, "But I am. So far, anyway."

When Logan lifts his head with pride and takes her hand, she feels elated.

"Well, ours is still very much a joint effort," Caroline admits. "We swap at every feed, but I give one of the girls a bottle while Travis feeds the other one. It seems to work really well."

"You're not breastfeeding?" Catherine asks.

Sounding a bit resentful, Caroline shakes a finger at her twin and scolds her for thinking badly of her. "Not everyone is able to breastfeed! I tried it for a couple of days and it was a disaster. I was getting stressed which seemed to be stressing the girls – so I sent Travis out to get the works; baby milk, bottles and a steriliser," she smiles over at her husband appreciatively. "Since then the girls have both been little angels and peace reigns in the Lovett household once again."

"If it works, I don't see anything wrong with it," Catherine states, surprising her defensive sister no end. "The main thing is that you and the babies are not stressed out."

Still looking a little uncertainly at Catherine, Caroline asks, "What do you think Adrianne will do?"

"Breastfeed, if she can," Catherine states confidently. "She's really into this baby lark – but now we've got the boys, I can kind of see why."

All eyes turn to Catherine and her cheeks heat up. "Well I can! Ok."

It is Travis who breaks the tension with a timely cup of coffee. "I always knew you would be a natural," he tells her while handing her the hot drink. "You have a nurturing nature; you look out for others without even giving it a thought."

"I do not!" she gasps, feeling like she's been insulted. But then Catherine relents, "It's just family, it's what you do isn't it?"

Smiling, the love shining bright in his warm brown eyes, Logan lifts the hand nearest to him and raises it to his lips. "It most certainly is. And you do it so well."

"How's the case going?" Travis enquires. "Is Emma holding up alright?"

"Emma's tougher than she looks," Catherine states with some admiration for her partner. "And she's been working really hard while I've been getting a routine going with the boys."

"So, you've started back to work already?" Caroline asks, not able to hide her surprise. "I don't know how you do it."

"If it weren't for Linda I don't think I would be able to," Catherine admits. "But now that she's living with us, and she's become Andrew and Adam's grandmother, things are going great."

"Linda? Do I take it that you mean Mrs Baines? And how come she's the twins' grandmother...I don't get it?" Caroline's brow creases in confusion.

"We don't have a living grandmother...," Logan explains, giving Catherine's hand a reassuring squeeze, "...so we asked Mrs Baines, now known as Linda, if she would do us the honour of filling the role and she was delighted."

"Well that's not fair!" Caroline states with a pretty pout. "Our girls don't have a living grandmother either. And won't it seem strange to the children, when they get old enough to realise, if your boys have a grandmother that isn't theirs too?"

Batting at Logan's hand, Catherine turns a scowl on him. "Why didn't you tell me that – now we have to ask Linda to be Sara and Leanne's grandmother?"

"And Adrianne's children...," Caroline reminds her, "...and she's planning on having 3."

"Good lord!" Catherine's jaw drops. "That means she'll go from 2 to 7 grandchildren almost overnight!" Looking down at Sara asleep in her arms, Catherine doesn't think Linda will mind somehow, but she might just be a little taken aback.

"I know it's a lot to ask...," Catherine tells Linda in an uncertain voice that betrays her inner panic, "...but Caroline seems to think the children will feel aggrieved if you're Andrew and Adam's grandmother and not theirs too."

All the way home from Caroline and Travis', Catherine had worried about what Linda would think about suddenly becoming the grandmother of 7 children. And no matter how Logan had reassured her, Catherine was afraid that she had inadvertently caused a potential family rift.

Then, before Linda can open her mouth to reply, Catherine goes off on a rant.

"I told Logan I'm no good at this family shit!" and she turns angry eyes to her husband. "You keep telling me that everything will be fine...well it's not fine, damn it! I've upset one of my sisters big time and the other will be once she hears how stupid I've been."

And before anyone can make a reply, Catherine storms out through the conservatory and into the garden saying, "I was better off on my own!"

"Oh dear...," Linda turns sad eyes to Logan, "...I didn't get the chance to tell her that I would love to be grandmother to all of the children. It would be an honour and a real pleasure."

Smiling at his onetime housekeeper, Logan says, "I'll just go and put her straight on that...," then a shadow passes over his lovely eyes, "...and a few other things."

When he goes into the garden, however, he has to search for Catherine. She's not sitting on the bench near the fishpond, which is where he'd expected to find her, and she isn't in the ivy covered gazebo.

Catherine, I swear you're the only woman on the planet who can make me feel so much love and anger all at the same time!

When he finally finds her, Catherine is sitting under a large tree in the furthest corner of the very large garden.

But when she sees him coming, Catherine is anything but welcoming. "Go away! I came out here to be by myself!"

Although his heart is breaking to see that his strong, wilful wife has been brought to tears, Logan is also angry. "Not on your life! How dare you say that you'd be better off on your own?! You have a father and two sisters who all love you immensely, and now you have me and the boys and you repay that by wanting them gone...?"

When her head shoots up to look at him, Logan can see the fear in her eyes and his temper evaporates. "What is it, Catherine...why don't you believe that you deserve to be loved?"

But instead of answering she lowers her head and rubs at her eyes and cheeks to erase the tears.

I'm not worth it, you'll realise that one day and then you and my babies will be gone...and I'll be left to pick up the pieces. And I've already started a family civil war...I'm just no good at this family stuff. I don't know how to make things right...

Sitting on the ground beside her, Logan pulls her into his arms and just loves her.

After a short while he feels Catherine soften into him and is relieved. "I love you so much, it hurts to hear you say that you would be better off without me and the boys in your life," he tells her quietly, and rests his cheek on the top of her hair then feels her head shake in denial.

"That isn't what I meant," she whispers, hardly daring to speak the words out loud. "I just know I'm going to mess things up...just like I did this morning with Caroline...and then you and Andrew and Adam will be gone...and..."

"That will never happen," Logan pulls her more firmly against him. "Stop giving yourself such a hard time; you've had to guard your feelings and arm yourself against the world because it dealt you a bloody poor hand. But that's over now and, given time, I believe you will come to know all about what being part of a family truly means and you'll be glad of us."

Not if I drive you away first and I'm pretty good at that! Oh God, please don't let me mess this up...I love him with all my heart and I think I can be a good mum if you just help me along a bit...please...

"I'm so scared...," she admits finally, snuggling into Logan and loving the comfort she finds there, "...I couldn't love you or our boys any more if I tried and I don't know what to do. I'm terrified of losing everything I've ever dreamed of having; it just feels too good to be real...or too good for me anyway."

Putting a finger under her chin, Logan lifts her face to look at him and leaves her in no doubt about his love. It pours from his adoring eyes and his lips lower to show her the depth of that love.

It isn't the first time they have made love in the garden, but it is the first time that the act has been so profoundly binding.

In every touch of his lips and every caress of his large gentle hands, Logan lays his heart bare. Without the need for words he shows her and worships her until there can be no doubt in her mind.

Let me love you always. Let me keep you safe and fill your life with joy. You were always meant to be mine, Catherine, and I'll keep loving you until the day I die, and even then...

<u>CHAPTER THIRTEEN</u>

"I've been going through our list of suspects and doing a background check on them, their parents and siblings for any signs of cancer in the family," Emma explains when the two women have one of their regular update sessions. "So far I've come up empty, but I'm sticking to the suspect and their immediate family for now and I'll widen it out if we don't get a good hit on any of them."

"Ok...," Catherine agrees, "...I think that's a good tactic. Though, if you think about it, this whole thing started because of how upset you were at losing your aunt...so let's not rule anything out of the realms of possibility."

"Your right," Emma sighs and feels the loss of her favourite aunt deep within her heart. *I haven't forgotten you aunt Izzy and I never will. We'll find out who took you away from us...we will...I promise.*

"Sorry...I..." Catherine berates herself for her lack of tact and worries that she has upset her friend and colleague.

"It's ok, I'm fine. It just hits me sometimes, the fact that I'll never see Izzy again – no more girly chats or sharing secrets...or just visiting because we were so comfortable together," Emma recalls wistfully.

"Do you ever think it would be easier if you hadn't had all that in the first place?" Catherine asks tentatively. "I mean, it obviously hurts you pretty badly that she's gone."

But Emma gives a bright smile and shakes her head, "Never. I wouldn't change a single moment of having aunt Izzy in my life, my only regret is that we didn't have longer – but I would have felt like that no matter when she was taken from me. I loved her," she adds simply.

"Give me half the list you've got left and I'll get started on doing some of the background checks," Catherine changes the subject abruptly and holds her hand out for the list.

But Emma can sense that something is wrong and doesn't move to comply.

"What's wrong...have you and Logan had words?" she asks with a concerned frown.

"No...well, yes...but that's not it and it wasn't his

fault," Catherine defends loyally. "I managed to upset everyone yesterday, which I know will come as no big surprise to you, but it scared the living hell out of me."

Emma knows that Catherine doesn't make these kinds of confessions easily, so also knows that her friend must be hurting badly.

"Come on, let's get a brew and take five," Emma crosses the room to the kettle and switches it on. "If we can't help each other then we're going to be useless at helping others."

Frowning, Catherine moves across the room with Emma and considers her throw away words.

"You really believe that?" she asks.

Turning to Catherine, Emma lifts a brow, "Of course, don't you?"

"I suppose...I just never thought about it."

Handing her a mug of strong black coffee, Emma watches Catherine walk to sit behind her desk and pulls up a chair opposite her.

"But that's just you, Catherine...," Emma states matter of fact, "...you don't think about whether or not you'll help someone, you just do it instinctively."

Feeling uncomfortable with the insight, Catherine shifts in her seat. "Logan said something like that yesterday."

"And you didn't believe him...?"

Pursing her lips, Catherine's brow pulls into an annoyed frown. "Since when did you become the psychic?! I thought that was supposed to be my province!"

"Stop changing the subject," Emma tells her knowingly. "Tell me what's really bothering you."

Not sure if she's angry with her friend or not, Catherine takes a steadying breath then lets it out slowly. "I've never been bothered about having friends or lovers or any of that stuff," Catherine finally confides. "But now my life is filled with family and friends and... Well how the hell am I supposed to know how to deal with all that?"

"And...?" Emma persists.

"And what?!" Catherine frowns, all her annoyance flooding back.

"That isn't what's bothering you," Emma sips her coffee and watches Catherine struggle with some inner turmoil. "Just get it out; I can't help you if you don't tell me what's really wrong."

Getting to her feet, Catherine begins to do her usual pacing as her anger builds and her thoughts collide. "I never asked Logan to love me, I never asked him to go meddling in my past to find my family, and I sure as hell never asked him to take me out of my safe little world and throw all this at me," she states, her arms lifting and turning to encompass not only the room she is standing in but the house and everyone in it. "I never wanted all this...it was only ever a dream."

Nodding, Emma finally understands, "And dreams don't hurt so badly when they fade in the light of day...?"

"Yes! Yes!" Catherine agrees, coming to a stop by Emma. "It doesn't take a genius to work out that losing the real thing is going to hurt like hell, so why doesn't Logan understand that?!"

Oh, Catherine. Why is it so easy for you to believe that it will all come to an end...that there can be no other possible outcome?

"Can you imagine yourself ever falling out of love with Logan or wanting to leave him?" Then Emma chuckles at her friend's horror stricken face and the frantic shake of her head as she stops midway to retaking her seat. "So what makes you so sure that Logan is ever going to feel that way? Personally I've never seen a man more in love with his wife. I'm sort of jealous, if you must know."

Then it's Catherine's turn to chuckle, only now it's in disbelief, "That's bullshit! You've got Sloane eating out of your hand. I saw the way he looked at you when you got upset and he hugged you."

Grinning coyly, Emma nods in agreement, "He does

seem to like me doesn't he, and he's great in bed."

Catherine splutters on the mouthful of coffee she's just taken and blushes to the roots of her blonde hair. "What the hell! Don't be telling me about your sex life, damn it - that's between you and Shivers and isn't proper office talk!"

But Emma is unrepentant and continues to regale her with even more details.

"Shivers...he really lives up to his name. I've never known a man to make me shiver the way he does...he's amazing..." she finishes dreamily.

"Will you stop!" Catherine tells her frantically. "How will I ever be able to look him in the eye without imagining you together if you don't stop filling my head with pornographic images of the two of you?"

"Ok...," Emma smothers a laugh and gets to her feet, "...but I just need to say one more thing...," and she watches Catherine eye her warily, "...orgasm!"

When Catherine lets out a gasp and covers her ears with her hands, Emma can't stop the explosion of laughter that erupts from her. But at least she's taken Catherine's mind off of her troubles for a while.

Both girls spend the next couple of hours bent over their laptops reading the medical files of their suspects and their immediate families.

Some of it makes very sad reading; one nurse had a dad who'd suffered with cancer for years. They'd predicted his death many times but the father of three had defied the odds and had lived for 5 years instead of the expected 6 months.

Another one has a dad who is still battling prostate cancer and he is only in his early 50s.

"Christ, I don't think I realised how prevalent cancer is," Emma pipes up after reading of a young sister to one of the nurses who is still battling Leukaemia. "It must be devastating to find out your little sister has Leukaemia – I know it was when aunt Izzy told me she had breast cancer. I really thought that was the end."

Not sure whether to offer sympathy or if that might tip her friend over the edge into tears, Catherine decides to keep the discussion business-like.

"We can use that," Catherine nods over at a surprised Emma. "Tell me what it was like to know that someone you loved might die – what your emotions were how you dealt with them and how you ultimately came to terms with the situation."

Looking a little uncertain, Emma begins to tell her tale. "Well, I was waiting for my A-level results to come through and wasn't at all confident that I had done enough to get to university.

I was so self-absorbed that I didn't notice the signs that something was troubling aunt Izzy," she recalls sadly. "I was young and stupid, but that's no excuse; it hit me hard when she finally did tell me."

"How hard – were you angry enough to lash out at others?" Catherine asks bluntly.

Frowning, Emma has to think hard about that question – it isn't as easy to answer as maybe it should be. *I remember the injustice I felt that my wonderful aunt was in mortal peril because of some god-awful disease that she didn't deserve to have. That sort of thing should only happen to murderers or rapists, not to my kind and generous aunt Izzy.*

"No, though I was very angry for a time," Emma admits. "And we have to remember that Izzy ultimately came through the illness – she had to undergo a mastectomy, but she was alive and well after the reconstructive surgery."

"But if she had suffered, if she had been in pain and sick from the treatments...do you think your anger could have reached a pitch where you might have taken it out on other people?" Catherine persists doggedly.

Again, Emma has to take the time to think about the possibility honestly.

I was so angry and upset when I found out about Izzy's

death and the fact that she needn't have died – would it have been worse if the treatment had failed and she had suffered the way Catherine described?

"I don't know is the honest answer," Emma finally concedes. "But then, maybe we aren't looking for someone who is angry. Maybe we're looking at someone who was deeply saddened by their relative's suffering; perhaps a carer who went through the agonies of watching their loved one gradually deteriorate, maybe suffering the kinds of pain and indignities that we can't hope to understand?"

"Yes...," Catherine is up now, pacing to help her thoughts gel, "...I think you're right. These aren't simple murders...they're acts of kindness in a twisted sort of a way." *Maybe they started out angry then moved on to compassionate. After all, they work in a caring environment...why do that if you don't care about the people you're looking after?*

Then Catherine's thoughts take a different turn.

"But what if they are angry? What if they took the job in nursing to gain access to vulnerable patients?" Catherine restarts her pacing, her brilliant mind going off on many tangents and quickly dismissing most. "Yes, that's a very plausible thought. It could be that the cancer was only a focal point, giving the perp some kind of justification for their actions. In reality, they may have been angry that those people were still alive while the perp's relative had died, or was or is in the process of dying."

"Jesus!" The thought gives Emma the chills. "That would make the perp calculating and devious to the extreme. Going to uni' to get qualified and doing all the practical training – do you really think anyone would do that?"

Nodding, Catherine turns to Emma and recalls some of the cases that she and Logan had had to read through in order to track down her mother's murderer, Charlie Edwards.

"And Edwards was one of the worst of the lot," she tells Emma. "He stalked his victims for a very long time before killing them. He stalked me for two years and I never knew he was there."

"Hell," Emma breathes the word softly, and watches Catherine walk over to a large whiteboard that has yet to be used. She takes the special black felt tip and draws a line right down the centre of it and begins to write.

"Ok, we need to write up two possible profiles," Catherine tells Emma, and at the top of one side she puts 'Angry' and on the other 'Compassionate'.

Coming to stand beside Catherine, Emma points at the

side with 'Angry' on it, "I'd list devious, calculating, determined and patient, on that side."

"You don't think those attributes belong on the other side also?" Catherine speculates.

But Emma shakes her head, "If the perp is being compassionate they probably started out in nursing for all the right reasons – they wouldn't have been so calculating or devious." But then a thought hits Emma, "But they might need those qualities to carry out the assaults without being detected," and she sees a smile tug at Catherine's lips.

"That's what I thought," and she writes the same attributes on the other side of the board.

Standing a little way back they consider what they've written. "We need to think how this person differs from this one," Catherine points to the two columns on the board.

"They might appear to be very different people," Emma speculates, and points to the 'Angry' side of the board. "This one might come across as confident, sure of what they are doing and efficient – while this one...," Emma points towards the 'Compassionate' side of the board, "...might appear submissive, gentle and very caring. In fact, they might just fade into the background moving almost unnoticed between the patients."

Her voice has grown quiet as she contemplates the reality. "She would be the more dangerous of the two, the one likely to get away with this kind of thing the longest."

After Catherine has written up their profiles she turns curious eyes to Emma, "You just said 'she'," Catherine raises a brow.

"Did I?" Remembering her train of thought she nods, "I suppose it was the idea of the perp being gentle and caring, we tend to think of that as a woman's role, don't we?"

"Yes, we do, but don't let that colour your judgement when it comes to looking at the male suspects," Catherine warns.

"No, you're right, every person on our list was in the right place at the right time – or at least had the opportunity to be," Emma concludes firmly.

Looking at her watch, Catherine realises that Andrew and Adam need their feed and her breasts have been feeling uncomfortable for a while now.

"I'm going to have to duck out for an hour," she tells Emma. "If you think of anything else...," and she indicates the whiteboard, "...just write it up there and we'll discuss it when I get back."

Helen Pearson is on the alert, with her head down and apparently filling in the patient's observations chart, she watches through her lashes as the ward's matron hovers nearby.

What are you doing...you don't usually spend so much time out here on the ward? And why are the Consultants suddenly always around – usually you can't find one when you need them?!

Moving to the next bed, Helen wheels the blood-pressure monitor nearer the patient and wraps the cuff around their upper arm.

"How are you doing today, Mrs Whitworth?" she asks solicitously. "I bet you're ready to go home soon."

Mrs Whitworth beams a thankful smile and nods her frail head. "I'm doing so well Mr Mayberry said I'll be discharged tomorrow," she declares, showing Helen how well her fractured wrist has healed.

"Sounds good. Now just relax this arm down for me and we'll get your blood-pressure reading," Helen tells her, then puts a finger on the touch screen monitor to set it working. "So will your daughter be able to look in on you each day?" she asks with genuine concern for this lovely woman.

"Oh yes, in fact I'm going to live with them," Mrs Whitworth beams happily. "I'll get to see my grandchildren so much more and, when I'm back on my feet properly, I'll be able to look after them when my daughter and her husband want a night off."

So, they're going to use you as unpaid help...typical! And no doubt you've always run around after them — that's probably why you were on the way to their house on the day of your accident. What kind of a daughter lets her 66 year old mother catch the bus? A damned selfish one, that's who!

"I hope you're not going to be getting around on the bus anymore," Helen observes while she takes Mrs Whitworth's temperature using the tympanic thermometer in her ear. "That was a bad fall you took when you stumbled off the bus and you were lucky to get away with just a broken wrist and severe bruising — it could have been very much worse."

Smiling her gratitude, Mrs Whitworth pats Helen's hand. "You're a good girl, but don't you worry I won't be doing anything as silly as that again. But I do like to keep my independence — I don't want to be a burden on anyone, especially not my daughter."

Holding the woman's hand, Helen gives it a reassuring squeeze. *Don't you worry, I won't let that happen. You're too nice for this awful world...you deserve some peace and I'm going to make sure that you get it!*

CHAPTER FOURTEEN

Breakfast in the conservatory is unusually quiet. Catherine is pushing her food distractedly around her plate and Logan is waiting for her to tell him what's wrong.

"Ok, I give up," Logan tells her, picking up his coffee cup and contemplating his wife over it.

"What...?" she asks, as if coming out of a dream.

"Exactly! What is wrong?" he asks, his tone brooking no denials or possibility that he might let the matter go with a lame excuse.

And Catherine knows better; if Logan thinks something is wrong she doesn't stand a chance of hiding it from him.

"I know you're busy right now...with work I mean...," Catherine begins tentatively, "...but I was wondering if you might schedule some time out to take me to see Faraday this afternoon – or whenever he can fit me in?"

"Neil Faraday?" Logan asks, surprised that Catherine has given him a second thought. *I didn't think you'd ever want to go back. Even though you agreed to see him again you haven't seemed keen to actually follow through...*

"Yes, I think it's probably past time I paid him another visit," she tries to smile. "I said I would, and it wouldn't be right to go back on my word."

Watching her intently, Logan notices that Catherine is having trouble meeting his eyes but decides not to push her on it.

"Do you want to give him a ring or should I?" he offers obligingly.

"Well, I can make it any time that suits, so maybe you had better sort out the time to fit in with your work," Catherine suggests, still not lifting her eyes from the plate of scrambled eggs on toast that she has barely touched and is now cold.

"Ok, I'll do that. And, Catherine...," he waits until she has no choice but to look at him, "...I'm never too busy to spend time with you or our boys. My family will always come before my work. Ok?"

Feeling awkward, and knowing that Logan means every word, Catherine tries to smile and nods her head before picking up her coffee cup and studying its contents.

Fascinating. Whatever it is you want to see Faraday about you're too embarrassed to talk about it with me. I'm not sure I like the idea that you could confide in a stranger but not in your own husband...hmm...

Apart from taking time out to feed and cuddle Andrew and Adam, Catherine works hard on the background checks that she and Emma have been running on the suspects and their families.

"Has Sloane told you if they've made any progress?" she asks Emma, leaning back in her chair to look at her partner.

"He said they're having another meeting with some of the bigwigs at the hospital today," Emma informs her.

"So, no new leads...?" Catherine persists.

"Not that Sloane has mentioned." Emma, too, sits back in her chair and looks at Catherine curiously. "Is something wrong? You don't seem like yourself today."

Expecting to get a sarcastic retort, Emma is surprised when Catherine only shakes her head then looks back at her computer screen.

"Ok, that's it!" Emma declares, and stands to walk around her desk and over to Catherine's. "Give!"

When Catherine doesn't look up but continues to tap

away at her keyboard, Emma clears her throat loudly. "I'm not going away until you tell me what's wrong." And standing with her hands on her slender hips, Emma's stance is quite forbidding.

"I don't have to tell you everything," Catherine states stubbornly, childishly. "And I'm the senior partner here, so you're not the boss of me!"

Not saying a word, Emma continues to stare down at Catherine, her brown eyes determined and unwavering.

"Oh for goodness sakes, get a damned chair and sit down!" And Catherine returns Emma's glare with interest, watching as her friend draws up a chair and then sits watching her intently.

"I don't appreciate being bullied," Catherine tells Emma, her tone belligerent and her expression angry.

"Then don't mess me around – I can see something is bothering you. In fact, I saw it the moment I laid eyes on you this morning," Emma states, not withering at all under Catherine's impressive glare. "If you'd just spit it out in the first place we wouldn't be at logger heads now!"

"Damn it!" Catherine snaps, then takes the time to calm down and pull her thoughts into some order. "I've been seeing things," she states, and watches Emma for signs that maybe she'll think she's crazy.

"Seeing things...?"

"Yes, damn it! Seeing things that aren't really there," Catherine snaps, her temper rising as she grows more uncomfortable with the topic of conversation.

"Aaahhh," Emma breaths, the light of dawning going on in her brain. "You mean you had a vision...was it about the case?"

Catherine frowns over at Emma sceptically.

"Just like that, you ask me if it was about the case without even doubting that it was real," Catherine scoffs, sure that anyone else would have thought her a loony tune.

"Are you asking me if I think you're lying?" Emma lifts a brow. "Or are you really asking me if I believe you have some psychic ability?"

Heaving a huge sigh, Catherine's temper subsides as quickly as it had started. "Both, I suppose."

Shaking her head, Emma can't believe that Catherine is still so unsure of her. "I don't believe you have a lying bone in your body. If anything, you're too honest for your own good," she tells her. "And as for your ability...it's as real as you are. It's you that has to accept that, not me."

Chewing on her bottom lip, Catherine is still reluctant to say out loud what her mind has shown her. "I don't understand what it is I saw," she begins slowly. "I know it was a woman but one minute she was just a bit older looking than us and the next she was an old woman of around 60 or 70."

Watching Emma mull her words over, Catherine says, "I don't know how, but I know it was the same woman, young and old – I just don't understand what it's supposed to mean?"

"Do you think it was the perp or maybe a victim trying to contact you?" Emma asks.

"Holy hell!" Catherine gasps. "I hope to heaven it was the perp – I don't want dead people popping into my head whenever they feel like it! Gees!" And she gives a dramatic shiver at the horrific thought.

"Then we really had better hope it was the perp," Emma sympathises, knowing that she wouldn't like the idea of it happening to her either. "So what are you going to do about it?"

"Do about what?" Catherine stares dumbfounded.

"Your vision – or whatever the hell you call it," Emma shrugs and sighs.

"Oh. Well...I'm going to see Faraday this afternoon," Catherine tells her. "Logan's arranged a meeting for 3 o'clock."

"Is he going with you?"

"Too bloody right he is," Catherine states firmly. "If

I'm going to delve into this woowoo stuff then my hubby is coming along for the ride!"

Emma actually laughs; Catherine's expression is one of someone about to go into somewhere dark and dangerous and who is very reluctant about it.

"You're scared," she grins over at Catherine.

"What?! I am not! I'm just approaching this thing with the caution that it deserves," Catherine defends, her spine stiffening at the dig.

"Well I'd be scared," Emma concedes easily. "It'd be stupid not to be. It isn't every day that you get to commune with the dead."

Catherine's frown is deep and her huff of returning temper is loud, "I am not communing with the dead, for fuck's sake!"

"But you don't know that," Emma continues, enjoying riling Catherine. "You said yourself you didn't know if she was the perp or a victim, so you might be communing with the dead."

Standing now, Catherine heads over to the kettle and busies herself making coffee.

"I know you're just winding me up," she states hopefully. "You don't believe that any more than I do."

"I think you need to keep your mind open to the possibility," Emma says more thoughtfully.

Turning, Catherine eyes her friend and partner to weigh up if she's being serious or not. "I suppose so. But I don't like the idea one damn bit!"

When Logan pulls the Range Rover onto Faraday's driveway, Catherine closes her eyes to steel herself for what she's about to do.

She'd filled him in on the details on the drive over, because Emma had advised her it would be easier on Logan if he was prepared. But she hadn't liked the speculative look he'd given her after.

He hadn't said he didn't believe her, or intimated that maybe her marbles were not all there, but he had remained quiet for a long time. And even now he wasn't saying much.

Neil Faraday greets them warmly enough; seemingly delighted that Catherine wants to meet with him again.

"Can I ask what prompted you to come?" Neil looks at Catherine, not hiding the fact that he's surprised she came back at all.

Deciding to be just as frank, Catherine lifts her chin and tells him about the vision she'd had.

"So now I don't know if I've got a dead woman popping into my head or if I'm seeing the perp," she sums up on a frustrated sigh. "But either way, why the hell am I seeing her as a young woman and also as an old lady?"

"I can't answer that, just yet," Neil tells her honestly. "But if you'll sit with me at the dining table we'll try to find some answers."

Logan had stayed sitting in the lounge the last time they'd visited Faraday. But this time he follows them and moves a dining chair a little way from the dining table so as not to distract them.

Reaching across the table, Faraday waits for Catherine to place her hands in his. "I want us both to close our eyes and just let our minds go blank," he tells her softly. "There's no time limit...just let yourself relax and your thoughts ebb away."

At first, Logan watches Catherine struggle to let go of her control, but then he sees her shoulders gradually droop and her chin lower.

I wish I could see or hear what is going on. They both look out of it; I can't remember seeing Catherine this relaxed without her being asleep!

He hears Catherine moan and watches her brow furrow as her back straightens. *Christ this is frustrating!*

Minutes later he watches them both open their eyes, as if some bond has been simultaneously broken.

"Are you alright?" he asks Catherine anxiously.

"Actually, I feel great," she tells him with a surprising smile.

"That was good," Neil proclaims, obviously pleased with Catherine's progress. "It will be easier from now on."

"What exactly will be easier?" Logan demands, his frustration evident in his annoyed tone.

Leaving it to Neil to explain, Catherine moves her chair to sit by Logan and slips her hand into his.

"Catherine has far more of a gift than I realised," Neil begins. "We managed to form a link that allowed me to see what Catherine was shown earlier, and more besides," he smiles his satisfaction over at her.

"So, what does that mean — you get to see her thoughts and memories like pages in a book?" Logan speculates, obviously none too thrilled at the prospect.

Blushing wildly, Catherine lets her eyes close.

"No, not really," Neil chuckles at his hilarious thoughts, but Logan doesn't look too impressed. "Sorry, but that really is a long way off the mark. It's Catherine's gift I'm linked into and so it's her visions and insights that I'm able to see and feel...nothing more."

When he feels Catherine give his hand a squeeze Logan turns to look at her.

Nodding, she smiles at Logan and says, "He's right; I don't pretend to understand it but I felt the connection and 'link' is a good word for it."

"Ok," Logan concedes. "So what do you think about

what Catherine has been seeing – the woman who is young and old at the same time?"

"Hmm...what do you think, Catherine? Is the vision relevant to anything you're involved with at the moment?" Neil asks.

Not able to go into detail, Catherine just nods and says, "Possibly. I have a list of people that I'm looking into who may have done something criminal. I suppose I could be getting a glimpse of the perpetrator – but why young and old?"

"If you were considering one of them a criminal, would it be the younger or the older woman?" Neil asks her to speculate.

"It would have to be the younger woman," Catherine states decisively.

"Then, is it possible that her mother is an influencing factor? Could she be the guiding force behind this criminal act?" Neil frowns, obviously intrigued and feeling frustrated not to be given all the details.

"That is a good lead!" Catherine points at Neil like he's just done something brilliant, and he looks very pleased with himself.

"Good. Good. Maybe I could help you to zero in on this person," he suggests enthusiastically.

But Logan heads him off at the pass, "Sorry. I'm sure

you would be a great help, but this is a highly confidential matter."

Looking crestfallen, Neil looks to Catherine for her opinion.

"Sorry...," she smiles apologetically, "...Logan's right. I'm sure you really would be a big help, but this isn't just up to me."

"Oh well," Neil shrugs in defeat. "So, will you be coming back for more practice with your gift?"

"I'm not sure...do you think I need to?"

"If you want to learn control and get the best from it you do," he tells her, just a little haughtily.

Realising that she has unintentionally slighted him, Catherine doesn't feel able to decline. "Ok then, if you think it will help."

Back in her home office, Catherine tells Emma all about her meeting with Neil. "I think he could be right...," she muses, pacing in front of the whiteboard with the list of suspects names on it, "...the younger woman could be the perp and the older woman either putting her up to the killings or maybe she's the one suffering with cancer."

"What was it like...?" Emma asks, fascinated by the idea of joining with someone else's thoughts. "Was it like Spock when he 'mind-melds' with a villain in StarTreck?

Catherine lifts a brow, "I have no idea what you're

talking about – what the hell is mind-melding?"

Opening her mouth to explain, Emma realises that she wouldn't know where to start.

"Never mind...just tell me how you felt."

But Catherine isn't sure how to vocalise her experience. "It isn't really like watching your thoughts on a cinema screen, but Neil was able to see exactly what I saw this morning. The memory just became crystal clear to both of us at the same time."

"That...sounds...interesting," Emma lifts a brow. "So, what would he see if you were thinking about you and Logan...you know...doing it?"

"For heaven sakes!" Catherine snaps. "Is that all anyone can think of? Sex is not the be all and end all!"

Now both brows are raised into her hairline, "So who else had the same thought as me?"

She wants to be mad, but the fact is Catherine had been frightened of exactly that happening.

"Logan was a bit... Well he didn't like the idea of Neil being in my head is all!" Catherine frowns.

"You mean he was watching?!"

"Of course! I wouldn't try anything like that without Logan being there."

"Gees, I bet that made him feel a bit weird. I mean, another man getting that close to you – closer than Logan in a way," Emma's voice tapers off softly.

Feeling really uncomfortable at that thought, Catherine turns the focus back to the case.

"Anyway, he seemed to think we're looking for a female and that the older version of her was her mother, who is either putting her up to killing off patients, or she might be suffering or has suffered with cancer," Catherine recalls while studying their suspect list.

"Have you got any females left to check on your list?" Emma asks. "I've only got a couple of males, the women I checked out didn't have any immediate family with a history of cancer."

"I've got two...," Catherine tells her, "...but they're going to have to wait a bit, it's time for Andrew and Adam to have a feed." *And I need to do something normal and grounded. This psychic stuff really gives me the chills.*

"Give me one of them and you can do the other when you get back," Emma offers.

Going into the nursery, Catherine gazes down at her boys and feels her heart swell. Andrew is already awake and staring up at the colourful mobile above his cot. Amazingly, Adam is still fast asleep.

Leaning over his cot, Catherine lifts Andrew and cuddles him to her then moves to sit in the rocking chair. "This will be our first solo," she smiles at her son as she places him to her breast. "Your brother drank so much earlier I think it's made him sleepy."

Snuggling Andrew to her, Catherine enjoys this time of individual bonding. She loves both her boys, but hasn't had much of a chance to spend time with each of them alone – her arms, and her breasts, are usually filled with both boys at once.

Maybe I can try to get a routine going where I feed the boys one after the other? I'll have to ask Linda about that. It's nice to be able to cuddle them properly.

"I thought you would be in here about now," Logan smiles, taking a seat close by. Reaching out, he strokes his son's head then reaches higher to cup Catherine's cheek. "I love to watch you feed them," he tells her proudly. "And you look much more comfortable with just one in your arms."

Nodding, Catherine shares her thoughts with him, "I was just thinking it might be nice to try to do this all the time. But Adam doesn't usually sleep so well – would you just check that he's alright?"

"He's fine," Logan declares, when he comes back to his seat. "If you think it would help, I could always hold one of them while you feed the other and then we could swap," he suggests. "That way I can be winding and changing the first while you feed the second. I don't think it would take that much longer that way."

Beaming a smile, Catherine's blue eyes are bright with happiness. "You really are great. I was terrified of all this...," she tells him, lifting a hand to indicate the nursery and the boys, "...but you and Linda have made it much easier than I could ever have hoped for. You're a really great dad, and an even better husband."

"I'd do anything for my family," Logan declares softly. "You are my world, my entire life."

When he sees a shadow pass over her face, Logan feels it contract his heart. "What's wrong?"

"You seem to have given up everything for us," Catherine worries her bottom lip with her teeth.

"I haven't given up anything," Logan declares happily. "All I've done is rearrange things so that I can spend more time at home."

At that moment, Adam lets out a whine then his eyes open and so do his lungs.

"Alright, alright...," Logan crosses to the cot and picks up his son, "...we hear you." And laying his son's head on his shoulder, Logan pats his back and walks up and down the nursery until Andrew is finished feeding.

"You see, this can work really well," Logan smiles when they swap the boys over. And putting a muslin cloth over his shoulder first, he lays Andrew on top of it and rubs his back.

Catherine is now enjoying her time with Adam. "It really is lovely to cuddle the boys properly when they feed. I didn't mind both together, but this is easier and I get to have some time with each of them in turn."

"It's all a learning curve," Logan assures her. "We can do this if it is better for you, or we can change back if you decide it isn't working."

But Catherine shakes her head, "No, I think this is good," she smiles down and strokes Adam's forehead and pink cheek.

Then her eyes go distant and the room changes. Pink curtains hang at the large window and the baby in her arms is wearing a pink baby-grow. *What the hell! OMG, the carpet and the walls...and...the cot has pink sheets...what...*

"Catherine? Catherine are you alright?"

Logan is looking at her anxiously and is relieved to see her eyes focus on him again.

"I...I think so," she tells him in a daze. "I just seem to have drifted off for a minute. I must be more tired than I realised."

But Logan isn't convinced, though he decides not to push her. "Maybe you ought to take a nap after the boys go down," he suggests.

"I can't right away," Catherine frowns at the thought.

"We're getting close to finding the perp, I can feel it. I'll be fine once I get back on my feet – this rocking chair just about sends me to sleep."

Allowing her to get away with the excuse, Logan decides that he needs to keep a closer eye on Catherine. "I'll ask Linda to listen out for the boys while I come and help you and Emma."

"You don't have to do that," Catherine declares, already feeling guilty that Logan doesn't spend as much time doing his own work as he should.

But leaning down, he gives her a kiss and a smile, "I want to. Let's just get the boys settled and we'll get this case cracked once and for all!"

CHAPTER FIFTEEN

Hours later, Catherine, Emma and Logan are still hard at it.

"This just doesn't make sense," Emma declares again. "This woman was riddled with cancer, had all the treatments known to man and didn't respond well to any of them – how the hell can she still be alive after all this time?!"

Catherine crosses the room and puts her hand out for the printouts that Emma is leafing through.

Ok, let's see what we have... The medical records are pretty clear, prognosis is terminal in a matter of days – so why isn't there any record of her death?

"Just give me some time...I want to look a little deeper," Catherine mumbles as she crosses to her desk and gets busy on her laptop. *I need to take a look at the official register of deaths – this could just be an oversight on the part of the hospital.*

"Tell me you're not about to hack into Somerset House again," Logan pleads.

"I am not going to hack into Somerset House, I told you before I don't do that," Catherine assures him. *But I didn't say I wouldn't hack into the online records of The National Archives and that is where all the records were moved to when Somerset House was shut down! Well...after they were moved to a couple of other places first...but that's by-the-by!*

It takes a while to get safely into the records and then to conduct a thorough search. But at the end of an hour, Catherine can find no death certificate for Mavis Pearson, mother of Helen Pearson and Health Care Assistant working on the orthopaedics ward at Langley Royal Hospital.

"Can you get Shivers on the phone?" Catherine asks Emma. When her colleague takes out her mobile Catherine continues, "Tell him we need to have a powwow at his earliest convenience. There's something really fishy going on."

Sloane Shivers is in his office when he takes the call from Emma. "Shivers," he answers abruptly."

"It's me...," Emma's voice sounds in his ear, "...are you busy right now?"

"Why, is there a problem?"

"To be honest, I'm not sure. But Catherine wants us all to get together here if you and Frank can make it?" Emma tells him cryptically.

"Has she found something?" he asks, coming to full alert.

"Actually, it's more about something neither of us could find," she sighs. "Can you make it in about an hour?"

Frowning deeply, Shivers agrees then pockets his mobile.

"I think Emma and Catherine might be on to something," he tells Frank a minute later. "They want us to show up in about an hour – I said we would."

"Did you now," Frank groans over the pile of paperwork he's been buried in for most of the day. "Well, if it gets me away from this lot, it's fine by me."

By the time they arrive, Catherine, Emma and Logan have cleared all of the paperwork pinned to the boards and moved it to a single board on another wall.

The main wall, which has two very large whiteboards on it, has been used to write up everything they know about Helen Jessica Pearson and her parents.

There is also a printout of Ms Pearson's ID badge photo, which makes her look like an innocent girl next door type. But Catherine suspects there is more to her than meets the eye.

Frank and Sloane stand in front of the boards and read the findings on them.

"As I would expect...," Frank smiles at the women with admiration in his eyes, "...the information you have gathered is superbly detailed and very well organised. However, you appear to be missing a certificate of death – is that why we are here, do you need us to get one for you?"

Catherine's expression goes from pleased to indignant in a millisecond. And Sloane Shivers begins to look annoyed at being summoned for such a menial task. *They could have asked for that over the damned phone! Bloody hell!*

"Well spotted," Catherine concedes caustically. "But as you can see, we didn't have any trouble locating George Pearson's death certificate – the fact that we haven't got one for his wife, Mavis Pearson, is because there doesn't appear to be one in existence!"

Then Frank and Sloane turn back to the boards and again read the information on Mavis Pearson.

"But she was terminally ill...," Sloane pipes up, and taking his life in his hands continues, "...are you sure you haven't just overlooked it?"

Standing to one side, Logan lifts a brow then actually feels sorry for Sloane when he sees his wife's reaction to his question.

Moving to within a foot of Sloane, Catherine's blue eyes give off sparks of fury, but her voice remains deceptively low. "Overlooked it! You think I just glanced at the files and 'oops' just overlooked it!" Taking a deep breath, Catherine valiantly tries to pull in her temper, "No, Shivers, we did not overlook it, the bloody record doesn't exist...got it!"

But Sloane again questions their findings, "You have a woman who was pronounced terminally ill around six years ago, how else do you explain it?"

"That, Sherlock, is why you're here," Catherine barks out, her voice rising along with her temper. "Emma and I have both gone over the records in minute detail – the death was never recorded!"

For a very long moment, while all around them watch nervously, Catherine and Sloane face off, their eyes locked in battle.

"I think we need to pay a visit to the Langley," Frank interjects, finally breaking the tense silence. "We need to get more background on this woman's working life and alert them to keep a very close eye on her from now on."

It is Sloane who eventually breaks eye contact with

Catherine as he turns to his boss. "Yeah, and we'll take a look at this woman's medical files and ask them what they know about a missing death certificate," he adds, pointing to the board where Mavis Pearson's history is written up.

Later that evening, when the two women decide their days work is done, Emma goes home and Catherine goes down to the lounge to find Andrew and Adam lying side by side on a baby gym that has colourful animals hanging down to entertain them.

"You look happy...," Catherine smiles at Linda, loving the family scene she's just walked in on, "...and so do they."

"We've been enjoying a bit of playtime," Linda chuckles as she squeezes one of the animals to make it squeak.

"They really seem to love it," Catherine beams as her boys both thrash their arms and legs excitedly. "Did you buy this?"

"Guilty," Linda's smile slips a little as she wonders if Catherine will mind.

But Catherine just leans over her boys and gives them both kisses. "You have a very kind grandma," she tells them, then turns to the woman herself. "But you mustn't spend too much of your own money – just tell us what you want to get and we'll pay, ok?"

With her smile fully back in place, Linda agrees, "Though this was a present from me to them. But if you want me to get a few more things in, it would be my pleasure to do some shopping for them?"

Looking askance at the very idea of enjoying shopping, Catherine says, "Ok, get what you think they need but have a look at the stack in the nursery first. We've had a few gifts delivered from my sisters and a few friends."

Arthur Kingsley and his wife had been particularly generous, sending a huge furry giraffe for the boys' nursery.

"And that reminds me, would you mind picking something up for Caroline's girls, I didn't get around to looking on the computer for presents," she grimaces. "Though why everyone has to go buying presents for babies that are not their own is beyond me." *The giraffe was a nice thought though; it looks lovely in the nursery. Good old Arthur, he never changes.*

"Would you like me to pick something up for Adrianne too?" Linda offers kindly.

But Catherine shakes her head looking dumbstruck. "Why would you do that...she doesn't even have a baby yet?!"

"But she will...," Linda chuckles softly, "...and we already know she is having a boy and he could arrive any time now."

"So, be prepared, is that the idea?"

"It is," Linda confirms, then turns to the twins when they begin to whine. "Sorry boys, we were ignoring you, weren't we. Here now, let's see what this one does," and Linda squeezes a small elephant that lets out a peculiar noise, making Andrew and Adam thrash their little legs and arms again happily.

"That has to be the weirdest sounding elephant I ever heard," Catherine grimaces. "No wonder you think it's funny," she tells her boys.

Turning to Linda, watching as she plays with the twins, Catherine feels a twinge inside her gut. Not jealously, but something she can't quite put her finger on. "I've been getting a few flashbacks to my childhood," she confides quietly, taking Linda by surprise, though she hides it well.

"Are they disturbing you, or are they happy memories?" Linda asks, not turning to face Catherine as she senses that she would be embarrassed.

"Happy, I suppose. It's mostly me and Caroline, just glimpses of us playing together." And then Catherine realises what the twinge in her gut had been. "I want it back — the childhood that we should have shared," she admits forlornly. "I look at Andrew and Adam and I know that I could never conceive of separating them — but my parents did. How could they do that?"

Turning now, Linda sees the anguish in Catherine's eyes and her heart twists painfully. "I'm sure it was a very hard decision to make. And we will never know the thoughts behind it, but you do know that your mother loved you deeply and your father never wanted to leave you behind."

When Catherine's eyes begin to glitter with tears, Linda takes her hand, "You've become the next best thing to having my own daughter – you are loved, Catherine, more than you will ever know, by me and by Logan, by all your family."

Family. I really am part of a growing family. I used to dream of this, of having brothers and sisters and parents that cared. So why am I feeling so down?

Allowing herself to be pulled into a motherly embrace, Catherine finds she can't stem her tears.

"I don't know what's wrong with me," she declares, confused and irritated by her irrational feelings. "I love my life now, so why am I suddenly so miserable?"

"Have you been having these feelings for long?" Linda asks, pulling back to look at Catherine.

Looking guilty, Catherine nods and turns her eyes to the contented babies still playing happily. "I love them so much, sometimes I feel swamped by my feelings. And Logan has been so good; I have nothing to feel miserable about. I'm such an idiot – I knew I wouldn't be any good at this motherhood lark!" And her bottom lip begins to tremble again as more tears threaten to fall.

"Don't you worry, you're doing a fine job," Linda assures her. "I think you've got a mild case of baby blues."

"What...?"

"Baby blues," Linda repeats, giving Catherine's hand a reassuring squeeze. "Lots of new mothers feel low for no apparent reason, but it doesn't usually last for long," she smiles. "Some doctors link it to the sudden change in hormones that comes with giving birth and believe it rights itself as the body adjusts."

"So, you don't think I'm going loopy?"

"Not at all," Linda chuckles. "I think you are doing wonderfully, just as I always knew you would."

"Ok," Catherine concedes, then leans forward to pick Adam up when he begins to cry. "Come on, little fella," and she lays him on her shoulder with his head snuggled into her neck. Rubbing his back, Catherine rocks to and fro until his cries quieten.

"He's fallen asleep," Linda smiles, then picks Andrew up when he lets out a big yawn. "I think they're ready for a nap."

The two women carry the boys up to their nursery and lay them gently in their cots. Catherine winds up Andrews mobile and watches as his eyes droop and close.

"I'm so glad you're here," Catherine sighs, her tears gone and her heart feeling a little lighter. "I don't know what I'd do without you."

"You would do just fine," Linda assures her firmly. "But I'm very happy to help out as needed. And being a grandma is more than I ever hoped for."

"So you're still happy to move with us to Lakelands?" Catherine asks, looking sideways at Linda.

"Is that what's worrying you?" Linda asks, suddenly realising what might be behind Catherine's shaky confidence. "I'm looking forward to the move – I think it will be amazing for all of us. And the boys will have a childhood that many would only be able to dream of giving their children."

Then Catherine does something that brings Linda close to tears and flings her arms about the older woman's neck. "Thank you so much. I love you too."

When Logan gets home from one of his forays into the office, he finds the two women sat companionably in the sitting room.

"Dinner will be ready in about half an hour," Linda smiles as Logan takes a seat on one of the large settees.

Putting a hand to his empty stomach, Logan grins boyishly. "Mmm, I'm certainly ready for it. I swear I could eat a horse."

"Will chilli-con-carne with rice do?" she asks, knowing it is one of his favourite meals.

"Ooohh...," he groans longingly, "...that sounds like my idea of heaven."

Catherine laughs at his pitiful expression. "You'll have to make good use of that gym when we move to Lakelands," she tells him, and laughs some more at his affronted look. "Which reminds me, are we any nearer to actually moving - I thought we were going to plan a visit sometime soon?"

Linda was about to rise and go check on dinner, but decides to stay for the update.

"Actually, dad says the builders are making real headway now that he's moved out of the house and they are working in shifts around the clock," Logan declares proudly. "I got a second crew on board, all working under the project manager and the architect, and it seems to be going really well."

"Your dad moved out?!" Catherine gasps in horrified surprise. "You can't throw him out of his own home just so that we can move in faster!"

Even Linda is feeling uncomfortable at the thought.

"No one threw him out," Logan defends himself quickly. "Dad offered to move into the gatehouse to allow the work to progress. He was delighted to do it," he insists. "Dad wants us to move in as much as we do."

With her brows drawn together in concern for Henry, Catherine mulls Logan's declaration over in her head. *I know he's really keen to have Logan move back to Lakelands, but to move out of his own home...* "If you really don't think he minds, then I suppose it's ok. But you make sure he has everything he needs in the gatehouse. I think we should drive down tomorrow and make sure Henry is ok."

Smiling, knowing that Catherine is genuinely concerned for his dad, Logan agrees, "But what about your case – it seems to be coming to a conclusion. Don't you want to be in on the final moment?"

But Catherine is already shaking her head. "It won't happen that fast. The investigative team will need to gather more evidence before they can charge her – so far it's all circumstantial."

"Then it sounds like we're off to Lakelands in the morning," Logan declares happily.

"Will you want me along?" Linda asks uncertainly.

"Of course," Catherine declares before Logan can utter a word. "We can take a look at the work Caroline has been doing on your rooms and make sure they're how you want them. If not, now's the ideal time to make any changes."

"I'm sure my rooms will be fine," Linda tells them, getting to her feet to go out to the kitchen. "Now, if you'll excuse me, I'll go and dish dinner up."

"Lovely!" Logan declares enthusiastically, causing both women to laugh.

CHAPTER SIXTEEN

When Inspector Frank Harper and Detective Sloane Shivers arrive on the orthopaedics ward at The Langley Royal Hospital, they find the matron and the consultants already in discussion about another suspected incident.

Having filled them in on the background, Mr Mayberry, the senior consultant continues, "So you see, there was absolutely no reason for Mrs Whitworth to die, let alone die so suddenly."

Frank Harper nods and considers all that they've been told and now feels it's time to act. "May I ask if Miss Helen Pearson was on duty at the time of, or just prior to, the death of Mrs Whitworth?"

The small room goes deadly silent as the hospital staff exchange looks of disbelief.

"Are you seriously suspecting Helen of being behind

these deaths?" the matron asks as if the very thought were an indication of Frank taking leave of his sanity.

"We are looking very closely at this young woman; we have a lot of circumstantial evidence to support the theory that Ms Pearson is behind the deaths, but no corroborating evidence," Frank Harper tells them with a look of determination in his eyes. "Which is why I'm going to ask you to suspend this young lady and also give us access to any lockers or other private areas that she may use?"

"Jesus!" In that one word the matron's Irish accent pronounced her acceptance. "I'll see to it right away – but don't you need some kind of search warrant?" she asks cautiously.

But Frank shakes his head, "No, all lockers, cupboards and cloakrooms that Ms Pearson may use remain the property of the hospital. So, with your permission, we are allowed to search them without the need for a warrant."

"Helen is on duty today; I think it would be best if we find an excuse to get her off the ward for a time," the matron tells them as she turns to the telephone. "Hello, it's Sharon Finlay here, put me through to Carly as a matter of urgency," she tells the receptionist.

For a moment she is kept holding, then Carly Fisher comes onto the line. "Sharon, is something wrong?"

"Yes, sorry to drop this on you, but you remember the situation we discussed a couple of days ago...," she asks, and waits for Carly to confirm that she does, "...well, we now have a suspect and I need you to keep her occupied while the police search her locker and any other areas they might need to."

"Ok, just send her over and I'll go through some personnel papers with her," Carly offers quickly. "But, Sharon, you haven't told me who it is yet?"

Heaving out a sigh, Sharon tells her, "It's the last person you would ever suspect – it's Helen Pearson, Carly...the police seem pretty certain of it."

Turning back to the men in the room, Sharon asks the police officers to remain there until she gets Helen off the ward.

"Not a problem...," Frank tells her, "...and thank you for your cooperation."

Moments later the matron approaches Helen with her heart hardened against her doubts. *I can hardly believe you would do such a thing, I've always considered you to be one of our most compassionate carers. But then...who else would I suspect of murder!*

"Helen, sorry to pull you away but I've just had Personnel on the phone – you need to see Carly Fisher, she has some forms that she needs to go through with you. It shouldn't take long."

"You mean right now?" Helen asks surprised.

"Yes, you can finish that when you get back."

Watching Helen leave the ward, Sharon feels her heart sink. *If I can be so wrong about someone, how the hell can I ever trust my judgement again!*

The search of the cloakroom yields nothing, but Helen's locker is a goldmine of evidence.

"This is a patient's own vial of insulin; it has their name on and should have gone home with them," the matron tells them when shown the locker's contents.

"There's more than one, and some other drugs also," Detective Shivers confirms.

"What about this?" Inspector Harper holds up a glass vial of Potassium Chloride. "Could this induce death?"

"Christ almighty!" Sharon gasps, and nods her head in confirmation. "This is a nightmare. We're going to have to review drug protocols and security." Putting a hand to her aching forehead, Sharon Finlay tries to keep her raw nerves in check and says, "I'll need an itemised list of what you're taking with you and, of course, Helen will be suspended immediately. I'll get onto Carly right away."

"I'd appreciate it if you just ask her to detain Ms Pearson until we can get over there," Frank Harper instructs quietly. "We'll be taking her into custody for interview."

But when they arrive at the personnel offices, Helen has already gone.

"I'm sorry...I asked her to wait in the waiting room for just a moment while I answered a call," Carly tells them apologetically.

Sloane looks daggers into the young woman but Frank is more understanding. "Not to worry, we know where she lives and I'm sure we'll catch up with her there." *If not, we'll have an APB out on her in the blink of an eye. We can't allow this one to get away!*

"What do I do? What can I do?" Helen asks her mother. "I only did what I was called upon to do...I helped those people. But the police won't see it that way..."

"Stop this nonsense!" her mother snaps out. "All you can think about is yourself, now pull yourself together and settle down!"

"Yes. Yes. You're right, this isn't about me...," Helen concedes, breathing rapidly as she climbs the stairs to the hospital roof. "What about my work...our ability to help the suffering...they can't be allowed to stop us?!"

Helen opens the heavy door that leads out to the roof and takes in a gulp of fresh air.

Her thoughts are becoming more and more confused and desperate. *I need to leave, to get as far away as possible. No. No. I can't leave mother...what will she do without me to care for her? Maybe I can hide? Yes, that's it, I'll hide in the hospital and I'll be able to continue my work.* "That's it, mother, that's what I'll do."

When Frank and Sloane arrive at Helen's house they are not on their own. A police van with two officers has followed them, ready to take Helen into custody.

"Hmm, no lights on...," Frank observes, "...maybe she didn't come straight home? Let's take a look round the back," he suggests when ringing the bell and hammering on the large door doesn't yield a response.

The back of the house is as much in darkness as the front had been. Trying the door, Sloane isn't surprised when he finds it locked. "Now what?"

"We have a warrant for Ms Pearson's arrest and reason to believe she may be hiding within this house – that means we have leave to access the property by any means," Frank declares decisively. "I don't see any sign of an alarm system – break the door glass and let us in."

Using a large stone he found in the garden, Sloane carries out his orders.

"Bloody hell!" Frank looks left and right but sees no sign of having disturbed the neighbours, but then they are not exactly right next door.

"Good job these houses are stood in spacious grounds – that glass went with a hell of a bang," Sloane smiles over at his boss in pure relief.

Using their torches both men search and clear the downstairs, then move cautiously up the large wooden staircase and along the uncarpeted landing. Taking a room each, they open doors and check for anyone hiding inside, then move on to the next until only one room is left at the far end of the landing.

Frank nods to Sloane who turns the door knob and they both rush in.

"Jesus! What the hell is that smell?" Sloane asks Frank, who is also screwing up his face at the stench.

"Over here," and Frank indicates the bed. "If it weren't for the fact that this room is almost as cold as a freezer the smell would be a hell of a lot worse!"

The two men look at the withered remains of a human body tucked up in bed.

"Bloody hell – do you think she murdered her own mother, or maybe it's someone else?" Sloane suggests.

"No, I'm fairly sure it'll turn out to be her mother. This is why there was no death certificate," Frank continues, and begins to look around the room. "She may have died of her illness; it was diagnosed as terminal. Or perhaps she was her daughter's first victim – the one that set Ms Pearson out on a mission of euthanasia for all those she deems are suffering too much to be allowed to live."

"So where is she?" Sloane looks in the wardrobe and under the bed, then moves to check behind the heavy floor to ceiling curtains.

"Everything we know tells us that Ms Pearson is a solitary soul – no living family that we know of and no known friends," Frank muses as he lifts a trinket box from the bedside table and takes a look inside. "She'll be scared of being discovered, but even more scared of being out in the wide world," Frank reasons, replacing the empty trinket box. "The only two places she feels comfortable and safe in are here at home and at the hospital."

"Then I take it we're headed back to the hospital," Sloane concludes, already heading out of the bedroom.

"This is Inspector Frank Harper...," he tells the dispatcher via his radio, "...I want as many officers as can be spared to meet me outside The Royal Langley Hospital's main doors immediately. I'm on my way back there to apprehend Helen Pearson on suspicion of murder. I'll brief them when I arrive."

16 officers are stood in a group to one side of the hospital entrance, with a growing crowd of civilians watching on curiously.

Taking out a photograph, Frank hands it to one of the officers and tells him to pass it around. While this is happening, he explains why they are there.

I'll need ten of you to spread yourselves out around the perimeter. Your job will be to apprehend the subject if she tries to make an escape and to stop anyone else from entering the hospital," he finishes, pointing to the men Sloane has selected. "Now get on with it and keep your eyes peeled!"

"Ok, you remaining officers come with us," and Frank leads the way through the main hospital doors then sends them off in all directions to hunt Helen Pearson down.

Moments later one of the Sisters from the Orthopaedics ward comes racing up to Frank and Sloane, "I just saw her. I just saw Helen headed up the central staircase – she looked deranged and if she goes far enough up it leads out on to the roof!"

"Point the way," Frank tells her, then takes off with Sloane on his heels. Taking out his radio again, Frank asks for assistance, "This is Inspector Frank Harper; I need a trained negotiator on the roof of The Royal Langley Hospital asap! Our suspect has just been spotted headed up the staircase that leads to the roof and is thought to be in a highly agitated state!"

"No, this way," the Sister tells them when Frank makes to open a door leading to the stairs. "We can take the lift to the fourth floor and then we'll only have one flight to climb to get to the roof!"

Following her, Frank and Sloane wait for the lift to arrive then step inside with the Sister.

"I don't want you putting yourself in any danger," Frank warns her with a stern look. "What's your name," he asks, then nods when she tells him it is Jenny. "Stay behind us at all times. Are you on friendly terms with Helen Pearson?"

"As friendly as anyone is," she replies. "Helen doesn't encourage friendship – she's a loner, prefers her own company...you know?"

"Yes. I just hoped you might have some sort of rapport that we could work with until the trained negotiator gets here," Frank frowns thoughtfully.

"As long as you're not at loggerheads, we still might be able to use you as a familiar face to relate to," Sloane suggests hopefully.

"Well I'm up for it," Jenny tells them. "That is, if she has gone as far as the roof – she may have gotten off on one of the other floors."

"True. True. But we'll check the roof first, just in case," Frank decides. "We can always work our way down from the top if she isn't there."

But when they step through the heavy door leading out to the roof a couple of minutes later, they see Helen pacing back and forth in conversation with someone that none of them can see.

"Stay back…," Frank warns them both, "…I don't want to scare her." Then he moves forward and calls to Helen. "You must be cold…," he suggests when she turns to him, her eyes round with surprise, "…would you like my jacket, my dear?"

As he makes to shrug it off, Helen shakes her head wildly and backs away.

"Ok, that's fine, we'll just talk," Frank suggests quietly.

"I don't know you. My mother wouldn't like me talking to a stranger. You stay back. You keep away from me," Helen demands, backing up dangerously close to the edge of the building.

Frank holds up a hand and takes a couple of steps back, "Stop, Helen! I won't come near you if you just stand still," he tells her, taking another step back as she takes one forwards.

"Don't you lie to me!" she snaps out abruptly, shaking a finger at him. "It's a sin to lie and you look like a sinner!"

"No, no, we just wanted to tell you that we went to your house but, of course, you weren't there," Frank smiles cautiously.

"You…you can't do that…my mother is ill, you shouldn't be disturbing her," Helen shouts, now pacing again, her breathing rapid and shallow. "Now I'll be for it...she'll be angry again and I'll get a roasting. You need to stay away from us," she demands, again pointing a long finger at Frank.

Helen continues her frantic pacing then surprises everyone when she comes to an abrupt halt and stares hotly at Frank. "You will leave my daughter alone," a stern voice demands. "You have no right to question and badger her this way – Helen works for a higher power than you could ever conceive of. Now leave her in peace to do His will!"

Taken aback by the abrupt change, Frank takes his time to assess this new and unexpected situation. "So, you are Helen's mother...?" he asks softly.

"Isn't that what I just told you?!" she demands haughtily.

"Yes...err...may I speak with Helen...," Frank asks amenably, as if the situation were not the least bit unusual, "...I just need to confirm that she is happy for us to leave. That she's alright," he adds when the woman before him just stares unblinkingly back.

For a moment, he doesn't think that she will respond, then suddenly her face softens and Frank knows that he is now speaking to Helen again. "Ms Pearson...?" he asks, and when she nods Frank smiles, as if welcoming her back.

"We understand everything now," he tells her, his smile widening. "If we had only known...none of this would have been necessary." Then he bows his head quickly in a mark of respect, "If you will allow me, I'd like to escort you back to your ward. Sister will ensure that your work is not interrupted again," he states confidently, and waves Jenny forward to back up his words.

"That's right, Helen. I certainly didn't realise how important your work is," Jenny also smiles, then beckons to Helen with her hand. "We need to get back to the ward, Helen. It's all hands on deck – we've had a few staff call in sick. You won't mind doing a late shift for us, will you?"

Helen narrows her eyes, then returns Jenny's smile, "I'd like to help out, but I need to get back to my mother. She worries if I'm late and there's no one to get her meals."

Looking brighter and more herself, Helen begins to walk towards them and Sloane and Frank move to either side to allow them through unimpeded.

"That's alright...," Sloane tells her as she passes by him, "...we called at the house and found your mother quite ill, so we brought her into hospital where she can be looked after properly."

Faltering, Helen turns to Sloane looking devastated

then extremely angry. "You had no right! You can't take her away from me. You can't! You can't! You can't!"

Before anyone can react, Helen rushes Sloane and catches him off balance, forcing him into a backwards run while struggling to stay upright.

"You can't take her! You can't take her!" she screeches wildly, driving Sloane nearer and nearer to the edge of the roof.

With split second timing, Sloane grabs the top rail of the metal steps that run down the side of the building all the way to the ground. But though he manages to save himself, Helen falls from his grasp.

Her terrible screams, and the sudden silence, will live with Sloane forever, he's certain.

What the fuck did I just do? Why did I have to mention her mother! Why didn't I just let her get inside and then arrest her! Now she's dead...and it's all my bloody stupid fault!

"Come on, lad...," Frank pats Sloane's broad shoulders then helps him to his feet, "...there's no point blaming yourself. No one could have known she'd go off like that. Helen was an extremely troubled young woman."

Back at the station, Frank leaves Sloane to write up his report and goes to his office to let Catherine know that the case is over.

"Bloody hell...," Catherine exclaims when Frank has finished recounting the evening's events, "...he must be devastated!"

"Yes...yes he certainly is," Frank agrees sadly. "Will you let Emma know...or should I?"

"I'll do it. You must be all in," Catherine adds when she hears his relieved sigh.

"It's been a long day and we still have reports to write up. So, thank you, if you're really sure you don't mind explaining to Emma?" he adds guiltily.

"It's not a problem. Tell Sloane I'm sorry. Bye," she finishes abruptly, feeling embarrassed by her sympathy for Sloane.

Logan has been listening to the conversation via the speaker, and he watches Catherine intently.

"Showing your feelings isn't a crime," Logan finally tells her when Catherine fails to speak.

"I know that!" Catherine snaps, then turns her blue eyes to Logan and says, "Sorry. I didn't mean to say it like that."

Crossing the room, Logan pulls Catherine into his arms and just holds her tightly.

Worrying at her bottom lip, Catherine considers her options. "She's probably only just got home, but I think we should go now and tell Emma before she hears it on the news."

Kissing the top of her head, Logan agrees. "I'll go and let Linda know that we're going out. She won't mind listening for the boys."

The Range Rover heats up quickly on their journey, and Catherine is thankful. "Hell's teeth, I can't believe how cold it is – you'd think we were in the middle of winter instead of summer."

"That's the thing about English weather, isn't it? We can get all four seasons in one day," Logan chuckles, every bit as glad as Catherine that the heater is on.

After a long silence, Logan glances sideways at Catherine and knows that she is worried. "I think Emma will be glad to have an end to all this; though I'm sure she wouldn't have wanted it to end with a woman's death."

"I suppose," she agrees noncommitally.

Another silence ensues and Logan pulls the car over in front of Emma's house. "What are you thinking?"

Letting out a long sigh, Catherine unclips her seatbelt and turns in her seat to face her husband. "I'm thinking that, if we were talking about Edwards right now, I'd be royally pissed that he escaped a jail sentence! What kind of a person does that make me?"

Shaking his head in despair, Logan takes her hand and brings it to his lips then continues to hold it. "Edwards is a different kettle of fish altogether. This poor woman was obviously not in her right mind and deserved to be cared for, not to have her life ended by falling headlong off a building to her death."

But will it really be enough...can it ever be enough? Emma's aunt is gone, just like my mother, and I know better than most that the heartache doesn't go away, we just learn to deal with it.

Time isn't the great healer that many say it is; just thinking through the pain of loss is too much at first, but gradually we break through the fog of grief and life continues. Never the same, never whole, but we continue and life goes on.

"Catherine, Logan, what a lovely surprise...I think," Emma adds as she moves back to allow them in and sees the bleak look in her friend's eyes. "Is something wrong?"

"We just came to give you an update on your aunt's case," Logan tells her when Catherine doesn't speak.

But Emma's eyes are locked on Catherine's and she sees the sadness there. "Why don't we sit down, then you can tell me everything."

It takes a moment, but then Catherine tells her all about Helen Pearson and what Frank had told her about their attempt to arrest her.

"Oh god, Sloane must be in bits," Emma gasps when she hears how Helen had fallen from his grasp.

"And the fact that she's dead?" Catherine asks, curious to know how Emma feels about the woman who murdered her favourite aunt not facing prison.

Shaking her head, Emma considers her feelings then says, "I'll never be ok with what she did, but I can forgive her. Aunt Izzy was the kindest, most loving woman that I was privileged and honoured to know and love – she wouldn't want me to harbour bitterness towards a helpless woman who wasn't totally responsible for her actions. In fact, I think she'd want me to feel compassion and pray for her eternal soul."

Back in the car, Logan drives them home in complete silence. Even when they reach the house, Catherine follows him quietly inside.

Opening the sitting room door, he guides her onto a settee then pours them both a drink and hands her one.

"I have a pretty good idea what's going on in that brilliant head of yours," Logan tells her, coming to sit beside Catherine.

"You do? That's funny, cuz I have no idea what's going on in my head," she scoffs and downs a large glug of white wine.

"You're comparing your reaction to Edwards with Emma's reaction to Helen Pearson and judging yourself to be less of a person because you still hate him," Logan surmises, and when he sees her wince Logan knows he is correct. "But there is something you seem to have overlooked...," and he waits for Catherine to lift her eyes to his, "...Edwards is not insane — he is pure evil and enjoyed making his victims suffer. You have every right to hate the man; I just hope, for your sake, you'll be able to let it go some day." *But he hurt you on a soul deep level and I wouldn't blame you if you hated him till his dying day!*

CHAPTER SEVENTEEN

The sun is cool and the wind even cooler as they arrive at Lakelands to a very warm welcome from Henry. "Here, let me help you," he offers, and takes a couple of the bags that contain the twins' supplies from the boot of Logan's car.

After a couple of trips, everything and everyone is settled in the generous lounge of the gatehouse.

"This looks bigger than I remember," Catherine observes as she looks around her. "I think Emma will be really comfortable here."

"Do you want a tour – we've managed to get all the rooms decorated and most of the furniture has arrived," Henry tells them.

As the boys are still asleep in their carriers come car seats, they leave them in the lounge while Henry takes all three of them off for a look around the house.

"Good heavens...," Linda exclaims when they explore the kitchen, "...this is my idea of heaven."

"You enjoy cooking?" Henry smiles broadly at her.

"I do, which is part of the reason I became a housekeeper," Linda tells him. "I get real pleasure in cooking for someone, and I couldn't do that when I was living on my own."

Henry nods, considering her situation. "Then it was a lucky day for my son when you made that choice. Logan has never enjoyed cooking and relied on take-aways and ready meals when he was at university."

"Oh I've seen many students go down that route," Linda chuckles. "But luckily, in my university days, I was in halls with a group of girls who were all into healthy eating, so cooking became a social event."

There are four bedrooms upstairs, one box room, two moderately sized double rooms and a master with en-suite facilities.

"Wow," Catherine's eyes goggle at the sumptuous family bathroom. "Is that a whirlpool bath?"

"It is indeed," Logan chuckles at her shocked expression. "I told Caroline that she should go for the best and not worry about the budget. She's been amazing, considering that she was pregnant with twins at the time she was organising all this!"

"Did Adrianne help out? I know she was hoping to help Caroline but she and Robert still have a lot of work to do on their own house," Catherine grimaces comically.

"You still don't like shopping then," Henry laughs as he and Linda join them in the luxury bathroom.

"No one in their right mind actually enjoys shopping," Catherine declares. "It's something you do when there's no way out of it, and even then I chose to do it online! Much easier and much more acceptable!"

"That'll be Adam," Catherine adds with a smile when she hears a sharp cry from the lounge. "I swear he has an alarm clock in his stomach when it's time for his feed."

When they enter the lounge, it is indeed Adam that is airing his lungs, though not, it seems, loud enough to wake his sleeping brother.

Unstrapping him, Logan picks up his son and speaks comforting words in his ear as he places him on his shoulder and pats his back.

"I won't be a minute, my shawl is in here somewhere," Catherine frowns as she digs through the large bag of baby supplies. "Got it!"

"Would you like us to leave the room while you feed him?" Linda asks.

"No, it's fine, that's what the shawl is for," Catherine smiles, quite at ease.

Draping it around her shoulders, Catherine uses it to shield herself and prepares herself to feed Adam.

It isn't long before Andrew awakes and Henry gets his chance to hold him.

"There now...," he croons softly, his deep voice kind and loving, "...give your brother a chance to take his fill then it'll be your turn."

Andrew isn't crying. Staring up at his granddad, his brown eyes look curious and intrigued.

"He's so content," Logan tells his dad.

"You were more like Adam," Henry tells him with a smile of remembering. "Your mother couldn't feed you fast enough."

"Well, I'm sure I just had a healthy appetite," Logan defends proudly.

"And that hasn't changed...," Catherine chuckles, "...has it Linda?"

"You have a fine appetite," Linda confirms tactfully. "No doubt your rugby playing takes up a lot of energy."

"Yes. That's right," Logan agrees quickly. "Plus I do still work out at the gym when I get the chance. And that will be much easier when we move down here."

"If it's alright with you two...," Catherine looks from Linda to Henry, "...we'll take a walk over to the main house once the boys have been fed and changed. It'll be nice to see how far along the alterations are."

"Good idea...," Linda agrees brightly, "...then Henry and I can have some time with our grandsons."

"If I remember rightly...," Henry grins over at Linda, a mischievous twinkle in his eyes, "...it's a golden rule that grandparents get to spoil their grandchildren. And we wouldn't want to break any rules," he chuckles as he bounces Andrew on his knees.

Knowing that the boys are in very good hands, Catherine and Logan make their way to the main house.

"I don't know why...," Catherine begins hesitantly, "...but I'm actually nervous to see what's been done."

With an arm across her shoulders, Logan gives her a quick hug, "That's understandable, though I have a feeling you're going to love it."

Heaving a large breath in, Catherine lets it out slowly as they approach the main door. "I don't see any skips or piles of rubble," she observes curiously. "But then, I suppose they'd be round the back anyway, seeing as the pool and the gym are being added to the back of the house."

"According to dad, the builders have been very good at cleaning up after themselves – once the main demolition and digging out phase was done," he qualifies reasonably.

Walking in the large solid door, Catherine again experiences the wonder of Lakelands.

"This place is so beautiful," she smiles up at Logan, then a shadow crosses her eyes. "I hope the alterations haven't ruined this old lady. She's so dignified yet homey and I imagine she has many secrets she could share if only she could speak of them."

"She?" Logan looks down at Catherine with an indulgent grin on his handsome face. "I thought 'she' only applied to boats."

But Catherine shakes her head, "No. This house has the spirit of a Dowager Duchess living within its walls," and as Catherine looks around her, she is nodding her head and smiling with delight.

"Come on, before you call up some spirit that'll shoo us away before we even move in." Logan steers her through a door off the main reception hall with its grand ceremonial staircase and along a meandering corridor that passes the large kitchen to the back of the house.

"Now then, forget what you've just walked through — this is a modern and functional addition, hopefully, sympathetically incorporated into the old," Logan tells her, feeling somewhat nervous that Catherine may not approve.

Expecting to walk directly into the gym or pool area

Catherine is, at first, disappointed to have walked into an arrangement of changing rooms and a shower area. "Not quite like the local baths...," she raises a brow at the plush furnishings, "...but then I would have been disappointed if it was. This house deserves only the very best."

"Then step this way and tell me what you think." Logan guides her through to the pool entrance and watches Catherine's face for her honest reaction.

Unable to hide her delight, Catherine looks around at the clean lines of the pool, and the yards of floor to ceiling glass that give a resplendent view of the gardens beyond.

But there is nothing cold or sterile looking about it. The lighting is soft and luxurious furnishings line the walls. "This is amazing," Catherine breathes, finally putting Logan out of his misery. "I could never have dreamed this up – it looks fun and inviting, yet sophisticated and grown up too."

"Caroline's influence," he tells her with a grin, more relaxed now that he knows his wife approves of the changes. "Let's take a look at the gym."

Walking her around the side of the pool and through a pair of automatic glass sliding doors, Logan again watches for Catherine's reaction.

"Good grief!" she splutters, goggling at all the machinery and weights set out in the room.

"You don't like it...?" Logan looks crest fallen, having felt sure that the soft furnishings and decor would have taken the edge off the fact that this is a room meant for a good workout.

"It's...it's...," Catherine walks around the room, looking warily at all the different equipment, "...it's a damn torture chamber, that's what it is."

Laughing with relief, Logan demonstrates one of the pulley systems. "You can adjust the amount of weight you pull against by moving this simple locking bolt to where you want it." And he pulls it out and slides it back into a hole further down the stack of heavy metal blocks, then he moves round the front and lays on his back on the bench. "Now you just reach up, grip these handles and pull them towards your chest," and he does a few repetitions to give her a demonstration.

Although he looks damned sexy in his jeans and snug fitting t-shirt with his muscles bunching impressively, Catherine still grimaces, "Like I said, a torture chamber. No wonder I've never felt the need to join a gym!"

Sitting up, Logan eyes his wife with a challenge in his eyes. "Yet you were moaning the other day that you felt all soft and out of shape," he reminds her. "Personally, I don't mind a soft woman to snuggle up with, but..."

"Soft! Soft," she repeats heatedly. "Of course I'm not

as firm as I was before the boys, but I'm not a damned jelly belly either!" With blue eyes spitting sparks, Catherine slaps Logan's back and demands, "Get the hell up, I'll show you I'm not soft!"

But as she takes his place and reaches up to grip the bar above her face, Logan warns her to wait, "You'll hurt yourself if you try lifting these, just give me a sec and I'll adjust the weights."

Quickly, Logan moves the locking bolt further up the stack to give Catherine a challenge but nothing that will cause her harm. "Ok, that should do it."

Eager to show him that she isn't 'soft', Catherine pulls on the weights and feels the motion right through her upper body. *Bloody hell! I was right, this is flaming torture, but I'm not giving in. He'll rag on me to Linda and Henry if I do and I'm not going to give him that opportunity, damn it!*

Watching Catherine rise to his challenge, Logan decides she's done enough for a first time, "Ok, take a rest."

But Catherine isn't done and just glances sideways to glare up at him while she continues to pull on the increasingly heavy weights.

"Stop now, Catherine, you've done enough for a first go," he warns, becoming worried that she'll overdo it.

Then he hears her counting, "Nineteen, twenty," she grinds out finally letting go of the pulley.

"Now you're all sweaty...," he grins down at her, then leans in for a kiss, "...maybe we should christen the pool?"

Sitting up, Catherine can feel muscles that she didn't even know she owned aching and thinks a gentle swim might actually be a good idea.

"Ok big boy, let's get you out of those clothes," she grins lustily.

Going back to the changing rooms, Logan grabs a pair of trunks from a store cupboard and Catherine does the same once he's told her where to look.

"Jesus, Logan, who are you expecting...the national swim team?" she asks, looking at the stack of various sized swimwear all neatly piled and organised.

"I like to think our future guests will have full use of the pool," he replies matter-of-fact. "It'll be great to have your sisters and their families over; imagine the fun the kids will have in the pool."

That turns her smile into a full blown grin, "Yes, it really will." And her eyes go distant with imaginings. *I might not set much store by money in general, but what it can bring is the opportunity to enjoy some real family time. I have a real home at last, somewhere to settle and grow old with a husband and children. I have a family.*

"You're all lit up...," Logan puts a finger gently under her chin, "...what are you thinking about?"

"I'm thinking that you are a very quick stripper," she tells him with a lifted brow.

"Comes with experience," he tells her while jiggling his eyebrows. "Of the swim meet type," he adds when Catherine looks taken aback. "Get your mind out of the gutter woman!"

"Hmm, I'm not sure that I want to." And she stands openly admiring his heavily muscled body while she changes into her swimming costume.

Then she takes off and shouts, "Beat ya," over her shoulder at him.

"You little cheat," he mumbles on a laugh. But he is grinning from ear to lovely ear when he catches up with her and reaches around Catherine's waist, pulling her with him into the pool.

Coughing and spluttering, Catherine had expected the water to be freezing, but is pleased to find it comfortably warm instead.

"You maniac – you could have drowned me!"

"Not a chance," Logan declares, pulling her to him. "Can you swim?" he asks a bit belatedly.

Lifting a haughty chin, Catherine tells him, "Rather well, actually. It's the one thing I enjoyed at school –

though I'm nowhere near your league."

Then he lets go of her and pushes off the wall with his strong legs, "Beat ya," she hears him call as he strikes out for the nearest end of the pool.

When she catches up with him, Logan is already relaxing on his back watching her efforts.

"If you cup your hands more you'll move quicker through the water," he advises with a smile. "Other than that, you have good form."

Sticking her tongue out at him, Catherine splashes some water over his face so that he has to stand up. "We can't all be champion swimmers," she tells him with a frown.

"In this pool, you don't need to be. Just have fun, Catherine," and he dips his head for a kiss.

When he lifts his head, Logan is disturbed by a shadow he sees in her eyes. "What?"

Putting a hand to his cheek, Catherine feels swamped by her love for him. "You are the kindest man I've ever met. You never make me feel stupid or inadequate. I love you so much..." and she surprises both of them by crying.

Wrapping her in his arms, Logan just holds on until the storm passes.

"I'm sorry...," Catherine eventually declares on a shuddering breath, "...Linda says it's probably just hormones and will pass in time."

Relieved, Logan wipes away her tears and smiles tenderly at his beautiful wife. "You should have told me you were feeling low. I can't help you if I don't know," he chides gently.

"Actually, it's getting better already," she declares, then rolls her eyes at his lifted brow. "It is! Now let's swim before I have to go back and feed the boys again. And we still need to look at the rest of the house."

For the next half hour they enjoy doing laps of the pool together. Logan keeps his pace to hers, pushing her a little when he sees that she's trying to keep up with him.

"That was great," Catherine smiles broadly at him as they stand together at the end of the pool. "Do the showers in the changing room work?"

"I was reliably informed that everything works," Logan tells her as they walk to the steps to get out of the pool. "We have two saunas and two steam rooms also," he informs her.

"Why two of each?" she asks as they walk to the showers.

"Some women may not feel comfortable sharing with male company," he smiles easily. "It was no trouble to have a second of each installed while we were doing such radical building work anyway."

"Considerate as always," Catherine declares while turning on the shower. Then they strip off their swimwear and step under the warm water.

"Let me," and Logan puts his hand under a plunger that dispenses a beautifully fragrant shampoo. Then he proceeds to wash her hair, gently massaging her scalp with his strong fingers in the process.

"Ooooohhhh," she moans weakly, her mind and body relaxing with his ministrations.

"Good?" he asks needlessly.

"Wonderful," she croons on a blissful sigh, then moans when his hands move to her shoulders to turn her more fully into the shower.

"You need to rinse off," he grins. "I'll give you another massage in a minute."

Then he proceeds to help her get the suds out of her hair, and while she remains busy he puts his hand under another plunger and gets a palm full of luxurious body wash.

"Oh my god, Logan," she croons, feeling his hands smooth over her shoulders and then his fingers begin to work their magic on her aching muscles.

"You did too much in the gym for a first time," he remonstrates softly. "You're bound to ache for a while, but this should help." And he continues to gently knead her flesh for a few minutes more.

Putting his hand under the plunger again, this time he smoothes the soap all over her back then reaches round to her belly. Circling his hands, Logan works his way up her body until he is cupping and kneading her full, round breasts.

"I don't think that comes under massage," she chuckles, then groans and leans back into him when his thumbs play over her nipples.

His mouth lowers to her ear, "I thought you'd enjoy a full body massage...just for medicinal purposes, of course."

"Yeah right," she chuckles again as she feels his erection nuzzle against her bottom. But her laughter quickly fades when a large gentle hand moves between her legs.

If he's trying to drive me crazy he's doing a good job. Damn he's good...

With exquisite pleasure, Logan explores her body and loves Catherine in every way known to man. He wants to give her everything, to show her that he worships her body as much now that she has born his children as he did before. She has a woman's body now, and he adores her.

<u>EPILOGUE</u>

The moving day was hectic but exciting. Linda was taking care of the twins while Catherine helped Logan supervise his men.

"That's great, Bill. Now, if you can take all the boxes marked CCSI up to the fourth bedroom along in the right wing I'll be up in a minute to start unpacking them," she smiles, tired but very happy.

"Are you ok?" Logan asks when he hears her sigh heavily.

"I'm fine. No, I'm much better than fine," she grins, wiping the back of her hand across her forehead.

Logan laughs and reaches into his pocket for a tissue. "Trust you," and he wipes at her smeared forehead with the tissue then kisses the spot he's just cleaned. "Maybe I should have left it; you looked like a real worker with smudges on her face."

"Cheeky git," Catherine laughs and pokes him playfully in the stomach. "I'm working just as hard as anyone here."

"You certainly are," he capitulates, then moves to kiss her when a subtle cough from the doorway interrupts him. "Alright, Frank?"

"Err, yes boss...," the big man looks sheepish if not a little embarrassed, "...we just need to get by with these desks and the like."

"Hmm, I think he's telling us we're in the way," Logan grins happily. "Isn't that right, Frank?"

"The desks are on the large side to be getting them around you," Frank evades tactfully.

"Alright, come on through," Logan tells him, and takes Catherine by the hand and leads her out to the kitchen. "Take the weight off while I make us a cup of well-earned coffee," he tells her while moving to turn the kettle on.

"I'm fine," she states indignantly, thinking he's concerned that she is tired.

"Well I'm not. I want five minutes alone with my wife," Logan declares firmly. "We've been at this since breakfast; I'm fed up of sharing you with a crowd of people milling around the place."

When he brings two mugs of steaming coffee over to the table, Catherine looks up at him adoringly.

"We'll have lots of time to be together now," and she

winds her arms around his legs as he stands in front of her. "Now that we're both working from home, we should be able to see a lot more of each other. Are you sure you're happy with that arrangement?" she asks, frowning up at him.

"There are bound to be times when I'll need to be away, but on the whole this arrangement suits me down to the ground," Logan tells her, stroking a loving hand over her hair. "I have everything any man has a right to ask for and more; if I have to make compromises to keep it then I'm happy to do so."

"Me too," she grins. "Now sit down and drink your coffee – we need to get back out there if we're ever going to get this move finished!"

The late August evening is balmy and quiet as Catherine and Logan sit on the grass at the edge of the lake. "This is so beautiful," she tells him as they look out over the still water cloaked in a silver sheen from the high moon.

"I've always loved this spot. It's peaceful and I can see my mother's cabin and remember her there," Logan tells her.

"Are you glad to come back?" she asks nervously.

"Very. You were right when you said this was home for me – I just hope you'll feel the same in time."

But Catherine shakes her head and smiles up at him, "Not in time, Logan. I feel it right now. I've always felt it, right from that first time we came here. It's like this place was calling to me, beckoning me home."

Then she laughs nervously. "I know that sounds completely cuckoo, but..." and she shrugs her shoulders unable to describe her feelings adequately.

"Then it's perfect. Our family will blossom and thrive here. Home at last..."

If you have enjoyed this book please leave a review on the site from where you purchased it. Thank You.

www.ingramcontent.com/pod-product-compliance
Lightning Source LLC
Chambersburg PA
CBHW070610170726
48291CB00003B/763